EARTH'S END
AN APOCALYPTIC
ANTHOLOGY

EARTH'S END

Cover art by Trevor Schubert

EARTH'S END

AN APOCALYPTIC
ANTHOLOGY

EDITED BY
ANTHONY GIANGREGORIO

Table of Contents

A GOOD DEATH

JONATHAN TEMPLAR

At some point since her unit was ambushed, Phinn had lost her watch. She had no idea how long ago that had been, or how long she'd been walking across what was left of her country.

For a while this troubled her, but eventually she shrugged it off. It hardly mattered now, the *Extinction Event* was closing in, and each heartbeat brought it a little bit closer. She had no desire to count it down. It was just a little odd to be adrift from time, to have no way of telling *when* she was. There was no daylight anymore; the sky was as dark at midday as it was at midnight. It could disorient you; leave your senses haywire as all the signals from nature they were attuned to had stopped transmitting.

Day and night, it was all the same now.

They had accepted their mission stoically, but they all knew it was pointless. The unit, hell the entire damn army, had been on 'domestic peace-keeping duty' since the Fall. It was tough work, facing down your own citizens, *gunning* them down on occasion, and it rarely made any sense. Their instructions tended to contradict each other on a daily basis, and the definition of 'necessary force' seemed to change by the hour and there wasn't a soldier in the country who could tell Phinn with any confidence exactly how the chain-of-command worked anymore. Someone came along and said jump and she jumped. No one asked too many questions.

Once she'd shot a few twelve year old US citizens in the face for looting, it was better if she didn't stop to second guess her actions.

The army was falling apart, just the same as everything else. The desertion rate was ridiculously high—high enough that nobody really cared anymore. Any serving soldier with a family had eventually been given the chance to go free and most had. That just left people like Phinn. The career soldiers with no home to call their own, let alone did they have anything for them.

So they'd all been given 'assignments,' each unit provided with a detailed mission with which to see out the end of the world. They were to go after the oil barons, those who had taken what stocks of oil and petroleum they could comfortably claim and declared themselves independent, outside of government control. When the oil stocks had run low, the army had suffered because of those actions. Now, at the very end, with little left to fight for, Phinn and her unit had been ordered to go after one of them, to take back property and possession in the name of the United States government. They were to use any and all necessary means to achieve this, and there was little ambiguity in *that* command. It was a simple mission of revenge, one with no practical purpose beyond one final 'Fuck You' from Uncle Sam.

Phinn believed it would be as good a way to die as any other.

There had been six of them when they'd set out.

Daley was felled by sniper fire from a rogue regiment shortly after they'd left the compound. He'd been young and foolish; Phinn barely had the time to get to know him but what she'd learned she didn't much like. Any soldier worth their upkeep knew that as soon as you left the military safe zones, you made sure that all your gear was intact and uncompromised, and you never, *ever* removed it if you valued your skin. The military had made many enemies in the days since the Fall.

Daley had unclipped his helmet, announced that he was going to take a last breath of fresh air if it fucking killed him, and exposed his face to one such enemy. The sniper had been an expert marksman, and Daley's head had exploded before he had the chance to take that cherished breath. The rest of the unit had little water to spare, even with the extra that Daley's death would give them. They couldn't afford to waste it washing off their buddy's brains. For days, bits of him congealed on their uniforms until the elements burnt it away.

The others had lasted longer. They'd completed most of their trek to the secessionist territories before they were killed.

It had been a pack of roamers, scrawny and disorganized but familiar with the terrain, who were used to setting traps and pouncing on unwary prey. They had dug out a pit in the valley the unit was navigating a slow passage through. Devon was taking point, and had fallen through the sticks and leaves the roamers had placed over the pit. The bottom of the pit had been lined with stakes, an ancient and obvious trap but a lethally effective one. Devon had fallen face downward, one stake driving through his mouth and out the top of his head. The others tore through his body, and though any of them alone might have killed them, together they simply destroyed him.

It was grisly but quick. Phinn almost envied him. It was a good death.

Before the unit had a chance to react, the roamers were on them, firing from above, aiming for the men first: Lawson and Welsh.

Captain Welsh went down quickly; even the bulky protection of his armor was unable to deal with the impact of multiple weapons' fire at such close range.

Lawson and Phinn had used Welsh's falling body as a shield and managed to return fire. They fought well; they were trained to do so, but they were in a weak position, and had little to aim at. Lawson took an armor-piercing bullet to the chest and then Phinn was alone.

The roamers retreated; they had what they wanted. They had Mahoney, after having managed to isolate and overwhelm her in the confusion. Phinn knew what the roamers did with women they acquired, knew what lay in store for her friend. Women generally didn't fare well since the Fall.

She saw the gang retreating, saw Mahoney being bundled away, her helmet torn from her head, hands pawing at her as they stripped the uniform away. Phinn took the shot and denied the bastards their prize. A mercy kill. Quick and painless.

Another good death.

And so Phinn was alone. The unit was gone, but she still had the mission. The world was about to end so she may as well carry it out.

She didn't have anything better to do with her final hours.

Phinn walked for what must have been days. She had enough water rations to sustain her but the lack of sunlight, the constant rumbling of the ground as the planet started to surrender to its own destruction, all left her disorientated and uncertain.

She was tired; her legs were moving mechanically, and it would have been harder for her to stop than to carry on. She would have loved to have removed her helmet from her head, to taste something other than her own scent, the saltiness of her own sweat.

But the air was worse now than it had been even days before, it was thick with dust and would coat her lungs within moments. She needed to find shelter before the filters in her armor clogged and gave up the ghost.

The outskirts of the town appeared before her like a mirage, suddenly rising from the dust. She staggered to the closest building, a shack that might once have been a service station or an automotive garage.

Phinn hammered on the door, punched and pounded and begged to be let in, the discipline that made her a great soldier lost to the dust that swirled around her.

Bolts were pulled back and the door swung inward. Phinn collapsed into the shack, and heard the beautiful sound of silence as the door was closed behind her and the never-ending wind was cut off.

She slept for the first time in days.

Phinn woke up on a cot, wrapped in a simple blanket that was more dirt than material, ripe with a dozen musty odors. She breathed them in hungrily, happy to have anything real to inhale after the stale, recycled air in her armor.

Her soldier's instincts were dulled. It took her a while to become accustomed to her location, to focus on the environment she had crashed into. It was dark, lit only by the hazy glow of battery-powered lamps. It *had* been a garage;, the dulled but still pungent smell of oil and the coppery tang of engines still lingered. The ceiling was high, with now useless strip-lighting running along it. There were shelves along the walls, and recessed alcoves that would have once held motor parts, perhaps. Everything of any worth had been removed a long time ago.

At her feet, surrounding her in a semi-circle, were an army of three and four foot tall dolls. Two rows deep, they had been placed around her like an honor guard. Dozens of strangely-painted faces looked up at her, each wrapped in a mockery of clothing of various designs, all pieced together with whatever happened to be available. Some of them were draped with old candy wrappers, the logos still clear. Others wore newspapers or magazines that had been folded and twisted into capes and hoods. None of the dolls had eyes; they all had hollow, skeleton faces, toothless mouths smiling up at Phinn, painted in lipstick and mascara.

"Awake then, are you?" a voice whispered from the gloom.

Phinn sat up straight and reached for her weapon. It wasn't there; she was dressed only in the sleek black bodysuit that lay beneath her armor. She felt naked without a gun.

"Identify yourself!" Phinn barked.

A phlemy, gargling laugh was her only answer.

"Identity yourself immediately or I'll be forced to consider you a threat!"

"Calm yourself, sweetheart," the voice whispered, and its owner crawled out from a hiding place and into Phinn's line of sight.

Phinn was immediately repulsed by what she saw, but relaxed her posture upon recognizing that the woman wasn't likely to pose any threat to her, armed or unarmed.

The woman switched on a lamp, illuminating more of the garage. What was left of the woman, anyway. She had no legs, at least beyond twitching stumps that ended a few inches from her waist. One arm was missing as well, and she pulled herself over to Phinn with her remaining limb. Her torso was resting on a wooden crate that had three awkwardly spinning plastic wheels beneath. Her body was wrapped in a shroud, her head covered by a hood, but Phinn could still tell that there were other parts of her missing too. One solitary eye stared out from under the hood, the other just a socket as empty as the dolls surrounding Phinn. Her nose was gone, but she smiled regardless, and still had a few teeth left inside her cracked and dry mouth.

"Where the fuck am I?" Phinn asked her.

"Don't you know?"

"I'm looking for what used to be called Fort Matthew. It was recently declared an independent oil barony whose adopted name I'm afraid I don't know."

"Well, I reckon you've probably found what you're looking for, sweetheart, though I know nothing about baronies, independent or otherwise. This is indeed Fort Matthew, or what might be left of it, and we do indeed have someone running things here who calls himself the Baron, though why he does so I can't tell you."

"I'm here by order of the President to reclaim the land and the oil illegally stored within these borders."

"On your own? And such a pretty thing as well."

"The rest of my unit are... following behind me." A necessary lie, Phinn considered. At least until she understood the way this place operated, and what form of life had developed here in the shadow of Armageddon.

"Can you point me to the man you say has declared himself the Baron?"

"Well, surely I will, sweetheart, but first you must rest yourself a while. I've made you some food, simple fare I'm afraid but since the damn sky fell there's little else we can expect. Wouldn't you agree?"

Food would be good. Rations had been sparse and unappealing for some time. "I'd appreciate that," Phinn said as the woman wheeled her way across the floor, towards a portable stove in the far corner. The dolls stared at Phinn as she waited, and she felt herself shiver despite her training. "The dolls. Did you make them?"

"You could say that," the woman answered while filling a bowl with a steaming spoonful of broth from a pan on the stove. "It might be more accurate to say that I decorated the little angels. I gave them some life and some color. It's my way of saying sorry to them for the ills that've befallen them."

"I don't understand."

The woman wheeled back, the bowl of broth resting on the crate before her. She passed it to Phinn. It smelled foul, and was a mixture of pungent vegetables and cooking oil with lumps of pale and fatty meat floating on top. Phinn didn't care, having already learned that any food was better than no food. She took a spoonful. It tasted worse than it looked, incredibly.

"You called them dolls, and I guess they are after a fashion. I suppose I treat them as such, anyway. But they ain't made from stitching and stuffing, sweetheart, those are bones that are lined up watching you."

Phinn swallowed another unpalatable spoonful and looked again at the 'dolls.' Of course they were bones. The eyeless faces, the empty mouths, these were the remains of children, the painted and decorated remains of children.

"Why? Why would you do that?"

"Why? They had such a short life, all of them. They was born and then slain, so best to make something beautiful of them, take what was left and dress it up nice. Make 'em look special."

"They were slain? You killed them?" Phinn's fingers were twitching, and she wanted the gun that wasn't there.

The half-woman looked puzzled. "Well 'course we did, sweetheart. How else were we going to stay alive when the sky fell? It's not like the cattle lasted long, no grass for them to eat no more. 'Course, there were many that didn't want to go through with it, didn't want to have their babies butchered like their livestock. But a couple of winters with empty larders and empty bellies soon brought most people round to the Baron's way of thinking. Those that could have children did, whether they wanted to or not. Those like me, the ones whose baby-making days were long over or hadn't started working in the first place, we weren't no good to anybody. We had to find our own way of surviving. I got what was left after they took the meat, to make my own little family. Sweet, ain't they?"

Phinn put down her bowl, unable to digest the foul soup as well as the information she'd just been given.

"You *ate* your babies?"

"Well, 'course I did! There ain't no meat as sweet as newborn." She licked her lips and giggled and Phinn realized that the woman was quite, quite mad. She could feel the terrible gaze of the dead army; could hear their silent pleas.

"The whole fucking town has turned cannibal? You know that's against the law? That any community found to be eating the flesh of their own is to be razed to the ground by Presidential order? Do you realize that?"

The woman waved her single hand dismissively. "It's been an awful long time since we listened to anything the government had to say for themselves. It was them that made the sky fall in the first place, sweetheart.

Poking their machines down where they shouldn't have gone, cracking the Earth right out from under us. What right do they have to think they can make laws for us; that *we* have to live with *their* sins?"

"There's no justification for eating your own young. You're not animals. You can't eat your own."

"What about you then, sweetheart? Do your precious laws not apply to you?"

"What do you mean?"

The half-woman nodded her mutilated head at the bowl that Phinn had discarded.

"Whatcha think you've been eatin' there? Pork belly?"

The woman pulled her robe from her shoulder, exposing her upper body. Her breasts were gone, and there was just scarred and mutilated flesh left behind, rank and infected, the wounds inadequately sewn up and barely cleaned.

"Told you, those that couldn't provide any young for the feasting had to find their own way to survive. It's amazing how much of yourself you can learn to live without. I always was partial to a nice piece of breast." She cackled with dark mirth.

Phinn felt the nausea attack her in waves, and she heaved and vomited everything she'd eaten onto the filthy floor. She could taste the foul broth in her mouth and her stomach continued to rebel. She retched until her throat ached.

The woman still cackled away, rocking on her stumps. Phinn straightened herself, wiped her chin, and kicked the woman off her crate. The woman sprawled across the floor, screeching in anger, in pain, or perhaps just in sheer insanity.

Phinn saw her armor in a scattered pile behind the dead dolls. She gathered it and found the concealed pistol hidden in the shoulder pad.

9

Without hesitating, she marched over to the mad woman, stood over her, and fired three shots into the back of the woman's head. The first bullet was enough to kill her; the other two were purely for Phinn's benefit.

Phinn felt much better with the gun in her hand. She dressed, then put the helmet back on her head. Her guns were gone, all but the concealed one. She left the garage and its horrors behind. She had business with the Baron.

As she opened the door, she could feel the movement of the earth beneath her, the ground becoming less and less stable. She could sense the planet screaming as it began its final death throes.

Time was almost up.

The Baron's men were waiting outside for her. She wondered how long they'd been there. Had her encounter with the half-woman been by design rather than an accident?

Had they known she was coming and made sure she had the appropriate welcome? On their heads it would be if that was the case.

There were three of them, standing and waiting in the dust, their faces covered in scarves, their eyes with goggles. They held rifles, obsolete projectile weapons that would be clogged with the filth that swam in the air and would be more likely to kill the man who fired it than his target.

Phinn wasn't about to challenge them. She raised her hands, showed that she wasn't armed even though the concealed pistol was back in its hiding place. She walked over to them in supplication, happy to surrender.

They would only take her to the very place she wanted to go if she let them.

The men led her to an SUV, adapted to work in the dust, the first one that Phinn had seen in working order for years. They pushed her roughly into the back, one of them sitting opposite her and pointing a gun at her.

They drove off, the headlights illuminating only a few feet ahead; even the brightest light struggling to penetrate the darkness now. The wind screamed as the SUV tore through it.

The baron's man pulled his scarf down from his face. His lips were dry and the few teeth that still rattled in his mouth were black.

He reached out the hand that didn't hold a gun and squeezed her breast roughly. Phinn shook him off and hissed at him. He chuckled.

"I am going to fuck you with everything I can find," he growled.

Phinn couldn't wait to kill him.

They drove for a while, and Phinn could see nothing outside the windows. The SUV eventually came to a stop and Phinn was hauled out. They were outside a church, a massive stone building with a spire that disappeared from view into the murky sky. Huge wooden doors were thrown open and she was marched inside.

It still looked like a place of worship. The vast space within was lined with wooden pews leading to elaborate stone arches, ornate glass windows unlit from outside but still breathtaking in their design.

The pews were inhabited by a congregation that had little to do with God, however. They were mutilated relics of what had once been a thriving community, addled by years living under sunless skies waiting for the world to end, and feasting on the flesh of their own offspring until many of them had brains that were little more than rotting sponges decaying inside their heads. Faces stared at Phinn as she entered, dull eyes and broken minds. Some of them drooled and seemed barely sentient, others were hooting and clapping as she made her way down the aisle, as if she were the darkest bride the church had ever known.

The Baron was waiting for her. He sat hunched upon his throne at the center of the altar. He was a giant of a man, and had seemingly spent the days since civilization fell pumping iron, given the size of his arms. He was bare-chested, wore black trousers and steel-tipped boots adorned with spurs too large to make sense. On his head he wore a leather mask, something appropriated from a fetish collection, the mouth a zippered flap, the eyes two rectangular holes. Four large rubber spikes protruded from the top of the mask like a crown of thorns.

He was a truly terrifying spectacle, and even a hardened soldier like Phinn felt hesitant approaching him.

The Baron held a leash made of barbed wire. On the other end of it was a man, naked but for soiled bandages that covered his groin and upper legs. He squatted next to the altar like an obedient dog. The man's genitals had been torn from him and were hung on a chain around his neck, both the cock and balls, now shriveled and dangling down to his hollow chest. The rest of the chain was decorated with severed fingers, and Phinn saw that these also belonged to the Baron's pet, saw the digit-less hands that balanced him on the floor.

The Baron raised a hand wrapped in a leather glove. His congregation fell silent, their babbling instantly ceased.

The masked face stared at Phinn. "It seems we have ourselves a guest. A comely one at that," he drawled, his rich voice like velvet.

There were hoots of crazy laughter from the pews.

"Hush now!" he bellowed. "Perhaps you'd like to introduce yourself, my dear."

"My name's Lt. Andrea Phinn, US Marine Corps."

"Well, it's very nice to meet you, *Loooo*-tenant," he stretched out the word, making rank sound like an insult. "And to what do we owe the pleasure of your visit at such a monumental moment in time?"

Phinn straightened herself and tried to look as imposing as she could. "I'm here under direct order from the President of the United States to take back the land you've claimed as an independent barony, and to take control of all and any property and possession that can better aid our country during this present crisis."

There was silence in the church, then the Baron laughed, a deep hearty laugh that echoed through the arches and was swiftly taken up by the crowd. "If you'll allow me to translate for the benefit of the less intelligent members of my community, I believe you're here to take back my oil."

"Among other things."

"Is that so? Well, Loooo-tenant, if you can excuse such an awful pun, you and whose army?"

The congregation hooted with idiot laughter again.

"The rest of my unit will be arriving shortly along with a significant artillery force, capable of razing this entire town to the fucking ground if you refuse to co-operate."

"I don't think they are, darlin'. I think you're on your own and you're telling me lies."

"Then why don't we wait and find out?"

The ground rumbled, more violently than before. Several windows broke and plaster fell from the high ceiling like large snowflakes.

"I though that would be your answer. I guess the end is very much nigh. Are you really that concerned with a few thousand gallons of oil, Lieutenant? There's little use left for it now, unless you plan to drink yourself to death on it."

"The oil is the rightful property of the government. This bunch behind me…" she turned to look at the congregation with contempt. "They're all going to hang and you right alongside them. You have no right to independence and you've surrendered to cannibalism. You're all just fucking animals."

"Oh well, I guess if you say so, Lieutenant, it must be true! You hear that, my friends? We're all just *fucking animals*!"

The crowd played along, making the sounds of the farmyard and the zoo, oinking and mooing and shrieking at their Baron's behest.

He raised a hand to silence them again. "You see my pet here?" The Baron raised the barbed-wire leash and the man at the other end of it yelped. "He came before me much as you have. He thought himself fit to lecture me on the error of my ways. He also told me I should be punished, that I'd blasphemed and violated his sacred temple. Ain't that right, Father?"

His pet nodded tamely.

"I tore off his balls and ate his tongue right out of his mouth. I considered that a suitable lesson for him. It certainly put our erstwhile priest in his place." He patted his unfortunate victim's head. "The question is: what do we do with you, Lieutenant? There's so little time left and so many wonderful things we could try. Or perhaps I should just give you over to my community, let them play with you while the world ends?"

There were ominous sounds of rising enthusiasm from the crowd.

The Baron was grinning beneath the black hood. Phinn could see his teeth bared behind the leather. She was ready to grab her gun, with one bullet left, and shoot herself in the head. A timely exit, but a coward's way out. Not a good way to die.

She had one last card to play.

"I challenge you," she said.

The Baron looked surprised…and amused.

Good. That's what he wanted.

"Challenge me to what?"

"I'll fight you. Me against you, for my life and for the right to lead your community. If I can beat you, hand to hand, they're mine."

The ground rumbled again. This time chunks of masonry fell from the roof, landing on empty pews and on some heads. There were screams, and clouds of plaster hung in the air. The Extinction Event was *now*; the Earth was shifting and in hours, perhaps less, the entire continent would be drowned beneath the sea.

The Baron stared, rubbing his chin. Then he rose and dropped the chain. He was massive, well over six feet tall and predominantly muscle.

"Very well. I accept your challenge. I'll beat you down, then I'll let this church ring to the sound of your screams as we torture you to a slow death."

"Works for me," Phinn said.

Without a pause, he launched himself at her. Phinn braced, put her weight on her left leg and then pushed back as he charged, using his own weight to unbalance him. The Baron brushed past her and sprawled onto the floor at the foot of a pew. There were gasps from the crowd. No one laughed.

Phinn turned, ready for him again. He rose slowly, powerful hands pushing him up. One of his flock was at the edge of the pew, chortling breathlessly, his shoulders rising with mirth. The Baron got to his feet and one powerful gloved fist shot out, catching the man full in the face, crushing his nose, destroying his face with the force of the impact. The man dropped lifelessly to the floor. There was more laughter, much more enthusiastic this time.

"Fucking idiot," the Baron drawled and turned back to Phinn. He was still calm, still in control.

She needed him angry.

He rushed toward her and she managed to deflect him again, catching him across his right shin and sending him to the floor. But he was up quicker this time, quicker than she expected, and was back at her before she could ground herself properly. He swung a fist, clumsily, and she ducked it with ease. He followed through with a kick which caught her in the hip and sent her spinning into a pew. For a moment the crowd had her, hands clawing at her face, tugging her hair. Phinn pulled away but left a clump of hair behind in a filthy hand. The pain stung her scalp and her eyes watered.

The Baron moved in. He swung again, she feinted, tried to go for the back of his knee, but he was ready for her, and grabbed her leg and swung her around. Her other leg slipped and she lost balance, and the Baron's strength was enough to send her crashing to the floor. She didn't have his padding so the impact knocked the wind out of her.

She looked up and saw his foot stamping down, and managed to roll away just in time as it slammed into the floor. Then he was on her. She felt his giant hand clasp the back of her armor and haul her up.

He put his arms around her and began to squeeze, the thick muscled arms tighter than any vice, and Phinn was trapped and powerless.

"I'm going squeeze you till you burst and your guts spill from both ends of you like you were a tube of toothpaste," the Baron hissed in her ear with a voice that was suddenly empty of the charm it previously held. It was now just as crude as the rest of the world he'd built.

Phinn closed her eyes, happy for it to end here and now without the pain he'd promised. She had lost, but she'd gone down fighting, as was her way.

Then the Baron's grip loosened and she was able to breathe again. She pushed away with everything she had. His arms let her go and she turned around, ready to face him once more, ready to fight. She was bruised and sore from his embrace.

The Baron was tugging at his neck, and blood was pouring down his chest, a trickle turning to a tide. He tried to talk, to shout, to *roar* his rage, but all he did was gargle his own blood.

Phinn didn't understand, couldn't see what had happened. Then she saw the barbs that were digging into his flesh, that had been roped around his neck from behind, then tightened. The Baron's struggles became weaker.

He fell to his knees and gave a hissing sound as the last of his life escaped his body. The corpse fell to the floor with a crash that made the old tiles shudder.

The priest stood behind him, the barbed wire leash wrapped across the stumps of his hands, bleeding down his arms where the barbs had torn his flesh as they had the Baron.

He tried to speak, but made nothing but a clicking, gargling sound as the stub of his ruined tongue rotated in his mouth. Phinn didn't understand. Then he pointed one ruined stump at the Baron's head. *At the mask.* He nodded enthusiastically and pointed to her.

Phinn looked at the crowd. They were shocked, uncertain what to do next. But it wouldn't take long. They would demonstrate their anger toward her soon enough.

She knelt down over the Baron's corpse and pulled off the hood. He was face down. She didn't want to look at him, didn't want to see who he was. Who he'd been.

The ground shook more violently than ever and the church rocked on its foundation. The end was well and truly nigh

Phinn pulled the mask over her head. It was musky, and the leather held the odor of stale sweat and the obscenity of its previous owner, but it was surprisingly comfortable.

It seemed to fit perfectly.

She turned to the crowd and raised her arms above her head in triumph.

They screamed with joy and love, and punched the air, hollering their worship for their new Baron, as the walls began to shake and the ground opened up beneath them.

All things considered, Phinn reckoned there were worse ways for her world to end.

It was a good death after all.

499 SECONDS

R P STEEVES

4₉₉

Beep

Dr. Berger was, once again and perhaps for the last time, grateful that he still wore a digital watch.

It was, in this day and age, something of an anachronism. With embedded tech flashing the time and temperature and coordinates and stock prices and sports scores directly across the retinas of most people, something as quaint and archaic as a digital wrist watch was seen as a quirky affectation at best and a sad obsession with the past at worst.

Still, he'd been wearing one since his youth and his wrist never felt the same without it. He'd worn a watch every day of his life, so it was only fitting that he wear one now.

But looking at it, he realized it wouldn't be right to sit there and continue staring at it as the counter approached zero. There was so much more he wanted to do in the next (here, he did glance down)…

476

… eight minutes or so. Unfortunately, that wasn't enough time for Dr. Berger to pleasure himself, which is something he'd always imagined himself doing in a situation like this. He figured the inevitable crying and screaming and wailing would not take as long as he expected, so that gave him time to do…what, exactly?

He glanced at the screens. They all showed variations of the same image and he knew enough to realize that, if what they were showing him was accurate, these seconds were all that truly mattered.

After devoting his entire life to this project and calculating all the possible scenarios and outcomes, he had little doubt that the truth was staring him right in the face.

449

He'd wasted almost a full a minute of the precious time, so after a quick glance at his watch — wasn't looking at the time supposed to make it go slower? So much for *that* theory of relativity. Too bad he couldn't write a paper denouncing that notion. Perhaps it would have been an easier ticket to the fame and fortune he felt he deserved, but alas, there would be no opportunity for any more academic writing. It's just as well. No one had listened to him during the entirety of his career, so why should that change now? People didn't deserve his wisdom anyway.

He stood up and stretched.

It felt surprisingly good. He didn't often find himself using his muscles. More often than not he sat at a chair or stood at a computer terminal. He found the movement somehow satisfying. The flowing of muscle and sinew, the tug and movement of his form against gravity. Just the motion of his body was exquisite. How had he never noticed that before?

He walked to the window and considered throwing up the shade. Maybe he could take the next few minutes and go outside — something else he rarely did, of course — and run and dance and move in the air until, well, until he could do so no longer.

No. It would be foolish to venture outside at a time like this. Even more so than normal. The walls of his apartment wouldn't provide much protection in the end, but it would at least be a psychological comfort not to see anyone else when the time came.

He leaned forward and shut off the computer screens. He had severed the remote connection immediately after he'd figured out what was going on, and leaving the disconnected screens active would do him no good. They'd merely serve as a reminder as to what was coming and how fast, and he did not need that. After all, he had his watch.

422

Still, there likely were people bustling around outside at this time of day, and maybe now, of all times, he should be with other people. But those he might meet on the street at a time like this were likely to become deranged or depressed or damaged rather quickly. The more time passed, the more people would learn about what had happened and how bad matters would become — and how quickly. Unless the fools never figured it out until it was too late, remaining ignorant until the end, which would be far worse than any other reaction, of course. Ignorance was never bliss, not even in a time like this.

Especially at a time like this.

He glanced once more at the screens, now dark. He could not remember the last time they'd been deactivated. They were such an omnipresent part of his life, always glowing, moving, and chirping. He used them for work and information and even for pleasure on rare occasions. He supposed that most people also used them for communication, and he mulled over that realization for a moment.

With whom would he care to speak right now, in this situation?

He could think of no one.

He had many contacts saved in his database, of course. It would simply be a matter of switching the screens back on and speaking the name of the person with whom he wanted to connect. But who would that be?

A colleague? Most of them were jealous or dismissive. Or both. He certainly would be inclined to tell a fellow scientist exactly what he thought of him or her, and that would either draw ire or merely cause the recipient to disconnect, so what would be the point of that?

He had no family. At least, he did not know how to reach any of his living family members, not without doing some research, and why would he want to waste any of his precious...

381

...seconds on research of that type? His entire adult life had been dedicated to research of one kind or another, but nothing so mundane as trying to locate a person. He didn't need people. It's why he'd created the AI in the first place, wasn't it? A mistake, of course, in hindsight. Well, perhaps not in its creation, but certainly poor judgment was shown in passing out the power, responsibility and duties; that was where the fatal error had occurred. But it was far, far too late to contemplate that now. Wasn't it?

So he had no colleagues worth contacting and no family of any real standing. As for friends, well, that brought him back to the AI option again, didn't it?

What colleagues he had met over the years — ones that certainly would not have understood his work or been able to deter him from his path — also would not have comprehended his design and deployment of the AI in the Astronomical Energy Analysis Array.

They certainly would not have approved of his rather tempestuous relationship with the mechanized personality of the robotic probe pilot.

Dr. Berger thought of keying on the screens and activating a connection with the AI, but thought the better of it. Even if communications had not been disabled — and the equipment not obliterated — what would he have to say to it?

He knew what it would deliver unto him if he gave it the chance. His creation was insufferable, to put it bluntly. He was determined not to spend these precious seconds, all…

345

…of them in an argument. Could it be that few? He shook his watch, as silly as it was. He knew better than most how such an archaic device worked—some of the circuitry he'd put into his Probe Mission had been inspired by such ancient technology—and he knew that shaking it would do nothing, certainly not fix the device or cause it to show a different number, save for the inexorably decreasing tally that was counting ever closer to zero.

His father had always treated technology in that way, shaking it, throwing it, hitting and yelling at it, perhaps believing that he could force devices to work through the sheer power of his will. It had never worked, of course. Maybe if his father had been successful just once, if his rage had produced the desired result in one lone case, reshaping the world into what he wanted it to be. .well, maybe then his father would have been a different man.

Dr. Berger mused that maybe he himself would have been a different person, too.

Again, it was far too late to think that way, and a waste of the precious seconds he had left.

Had he really wasted more than two minutes? Where had the time gone? Sucked into a black hole, it seemed, which drew in light, hope and time with neither care nor discernment.

The thought made him chuckle for a moment. The thought of sucking in all the light was a funny one. Very soon, there would be an abundance of light. An over abundance, in a manner of speaking. He could use a black hole right now. Or at least a wormhole. But, alas, there was nowhere to go, and in a matter of seconds, it would matter little where he was.

Dr. Berger knew he wouldn't be laughing.

303

He needed to get out of his own head. He needed to stretch his body and legs again. He needed to use these seconds wisely. He had never felt the pressure of time before. It had never been a factor, working for himself, using his family fortune, which had been left to him upon his father's death — no thanks to the old man himself, of course.

Mr. Berger — for he'd had no more time for schooling and academics than he had for his son, or apparently, lawyers — had never made a last will and testament. Dr. Berger assumed that his father had strong feelings on the matter, likely despising lawyers in the same way he despised doctors, environmentalists and scientists or anyone he considered a member of the 'intellectual elite.'

So, in the absence of a will, the family fortune, built as it was, on the shadiest and darkest of financial foundations, was transferred from father to son. The lack of a will had worked in Dr. Berger's favor in more ways than one. Had his father bothered to set down in a legal document his intentions for his blood money, the younger Berger never would have seen a cent of it.

The lack of a will had, he felt in a private and honest moment, made the authorities spend less time looking into the 'accident,' as they could find no clear motive, no one who would stand to gain from the businessman's untimely death by asphyxiation during, well, a rather private act.

Certainly no one looked twice at the shy, bookish son who spent all his time buried in a theoretical world, tinkering with thoughts of robotics and artificial intelligence, of propulsion and cold fusion and ways to harness the power of the heavens.

Either way, once the old man had passed, his fortune had fallen to the son, who never had to work for any master, nor answer to anyone scientifically or ethically, which freed him to create whatever he wanted in order to better mankind, to solve the energy crisis and usher in a new era of humanity.

Well, best intentions and all that…

269

But now Dr. Berger scolded himself. He vowed that he would never let guilt creep into his thoughts. He knew the truth about what he had done. He knew the reasons for his decisions and he knew his logic had been sound. He had no cause for guilt and no one to whom he had to answer, in this world or the next.

If there was one left...

That was something else that Dr. Berger had sworn never to do, especially in a situation such as this. He'd been raised in a religious environment. One, he might admit in a moment of honesty — and when had he ever been anything but honest with himself and the world? — that had been far too oppressive, which had led to his rejection of organized religion in his adult years. It did not — he would argue — lead to a moral vacuum, as some of his laughably labeled 'intellectual peers' had once said about him.

Dr. Berger had always believed that it had given him clarity of thought and purpose. His rejection of the common belief structure of his people and his time had allowed him to think creatively about issues, to develop solutions to problems of the day, like the energy crisis. It had freed him to follow a path that would have set him up to be the savior of humanity.

Though, he supposed now, that there had been a fine line attached to that label, and perhaps he had smudged it more than a little bit.

Enough musing. He had never been prone to introspection before, and had never given much thought to circumstances or consequences, living not in the past but in the far future, the oppressive present merely an inconvenience that lay between him and the glory and salvation that he knew he was ready and equipped to bestow unto the world. But all he had now, of course, was the present. Exactly...

221

...seconds of it.

Well over half the allotted time had passed away. He'd been given nearly five hundred seconds and he had squandered more than fifty percent of it. He wanted to go back, to hit the stop button on his digital watch, to re-enter the four hundred and ninety-nine seconds and hit the button again, to hear that familiar beep which had accompanied so many of his trials and experiments just one more time.

Actually, the thought occurred to him suddenly, he would hear more beeps, a rapid series of them, in fact, when the timer reached zero. At least, he presumed he'd hear those beeps. He tried to imagine, for a moment, what those final seconds would be like for him, for everyone. The four hundred and ninety-nine seconds was a rounding, of course, and he'd hit the start button on the count-down timer perhaps a few seconds after he'd learned the terrible news. Though the fact that he'd had the foresight to pre-program that exact number into his watch in preparation for just this eventuality probably would have told a more psychologically-focused individual that Dr. Berger had anticipated the worst, and indeed had prepared for it.

His brain began to imagine what had happened in the intervening seconds since activating the timer. He pictured in his mind's eye what he thought was occurring out there in the world, and what would happen subsequently, but he shook his head, in much the same way he had shaken his watch earlier. Not to get his brain to work, but to banish the graphic and tragic images that were starting to creep into his thoughts.

He needed to clear his head. He needed to make the best use of the remaining...

189

...seconds.

What then, would take his mind off of the dwindling seconds, off his creeping… not guilt, he'd never felt that before in his life and was certainly not going to succumb to it now. What was another word for the same feeling, only milder and contested by the facts and his conscience?

Dr. Berger pounded a fist on the table, his screens jumping a fraction of an inch into the air, as if startled by his uncharacteristic physical and emotional outburst. He'd never been good with words. They'd never come easily to him. He'd never known how to express himself, what to say nor when to say it, to anyone, neither his father, his rivals, nor *her*…

He cursed himself aloud. At least here was a word—or a stream of words, each one viler than the last—that was familiar to him. Oaths had come easily to his lips throughout his life, the one and only outlet for frustration and disappointment that gave him comfort. His father had not reacted well whenever he heard those words pouring forth from his only son's mouth, but even the belt had not cured the boy of the bad habit.

She almost had, though. Almost.

She'd always chided him gently when his speech pattern had devolved into a stream of guttural, almost pre-lingual curses. She'd reacted with bemusement and humor, showing far more patience with him and his bad habit than he ever had with himself and his own shortcomings.

For the five hundredth time, he wished she'd let him program the AI after her brain patterns. Perhaps then he wouldn't have been forced to use his own mind, and he would have been able to avoid getting stuck with a counterpart that was as stubborn and temperamental as himself. But by the time he had reached that stage of the process, she was long gone, so far beyond his reach that he would rather not think of it. Of her.

In fact, he never wanted to think of her again, and in a matter of seconds…

154

…of them to be precise, it would no longer be an issue.

This was all wrong. Everything about this was wrong. With less than three minutes left, he had done nothing with his time but self-flagellation, guilt tripping, introspection and wallowing in the mire of his own mind.

But, as he considered that, he realized how fitting it was. He was not the type of person to go outside into the fresh — though in the hyper-polluted state of the modern world, that term was certainly outdated and perhaps laughable — air, nor to reach out to another human being, nor to take part in any activity outside of his comfort zone. *His* comfort zone was squarely inside his mind.

It's where he lived, worked and played. Occasionally, of course, he would have to interact with his screens, perform experiments or analyze data, but he was too frightened to activate those screens now. He feared they would show him data that would chill his very bones. If he confirmed the approach of the looming catastrophe, if the figures and readings concurred with what he knew to be true, well, that would just make matters more unbearable than they already were. In that case he feared his introspection would darken further and he might just blame himself.

He had been only trying to do the right thing. He knew that to be indisputable fact, and if on the off chance that there was something waiting for him afterward, some ultimate judgment, some weighing of one's soul and actions in life in the beyond, well, he was confident that his intentions would outweigh his errors.

He'd only been trying to make the world a better place, to give everyone the gift of unlimited energy and artificially intelligent servants. He'd created the ship, programmed the pilot and laid out the parameters to try and unlock the secrets of fusion once and for all. He had never, ever anticipated what the AI would do up there, as it approached the sun. He certainly never imagined it would come to this, with him locked in his own office, the only one who knew for sure what was coming, the only one who knew how many seconds he—indeed everyone—had left.

That was…

112

…seconds. Just under two minutes to go until…

He looked around the room. What should he do with his final two minutes on Earth? What would anyone else be doing if they knew? Did they even know? Had the other so-called scientists figured out what he had done? No, he had done nothing wrong. It had been the AI that had decided to turn a research mission into genocide. Had his rivals figured out what had gone wrong and warned the world? Had they calculated the number of seconds humanity had left just as he had?

Were people around the world frantically making love? Declaring the innermost feelings they had suppressed for so long? Telling the truth to the most important people in their lives? Performing some act they had never done before but always wanted to do? Were people laughing, crying, praying or pleading with the heavens?

Had Dr. Berger, in his hubris, provided the rest of the human race with one last concentrated moment in time, one perfect, crystal-clear slice of *now* to take as their own, finally living their lives, doing what they had always wanted to do, what they had meant to do?

Had he given humanity the greatest gift of all? The gift of clarity? Of opportunity? Is that how he would be remembered?

He shook his head. No. He would not be remembered. No one would, of course. There wasn't even a chance that some space-faring race would someday come across remnants of the human race and study them as an astro-anthropological curiosity. Not after the planet was atomized in an enormous surge of atomic energy, turning the Earth into far less than a cinder in an instant.

Well, once the energy wave arrived, that is. Then it would be instantaneous, but that would not happen for approximately…

69

…seconds.

Approaching one minute left in the entirety of human history.

In some ways, it was too bad that no one would know his name. After all, even though names like Hitler and Stalin were spoken with derision and condemnation, at least they were remembered, and they had only been responsible for the deaths of millions. If their names were known by all the world, what sort of legacy would the man who killed billions, who was responsible for the death of the entire human race, for all life on the planet, in fact, have?

Dr. Berger would finally have received the recognition he so craved. As they say, there is no such thing as bad publicity and being the most important human being in the history of the planet had to account for something.

It was cold comfort now in the final seconds of his and everyone else's existence.

As a child, he had always found the naïve and overly simplistic notion that people should 'live every day like it was their last one on Earth to be laughable. After all, in that situation, most people would spend all their money and live with complete hedonism. Or perhaps they would spend the day crying and gnashing their teeth and cursing the fates and the gods. Either way, who would want to live every day of their lives like that?

But now it was a reality. It was the final day of life for everyone on the planet. The final…

31

…seconds. How would he spend those final seconds? What would it say about him as a scientist, a man and a human being?

Did it matter? Did any of it really matter? Most people lived their entire lives having no discernable impact on the human race one way or another. Dr. Berger didn't want to live like that. He'd wanted to save the environment and provide limitless energy, like the sun, to all. He'd wanted to create life, artificial life, to match his intellect and provide him company. He'd wanted to leave the world a different place than it was when he entered it, covered in slime and wailing his first breaths.

He had of course, made a difference. His spacecraft, piloted by his AI robot had, rather than merely gathering data on the sun, decided to sabotage it, opting to wipe out its creator and every creature like him, hyper-igniting the star and sending a wave of energy traveling at over two hundred miles per second directly toward the Earth.

Dr. Berger had quickly realized what was happening and started the countdown timer on his watch, marking the four hundred and ninety-nine seconds that it would take the energy wave to reach the Earth, traveling at the speed of light. He supposed he had always anticipated this outcome, knowing that the AI, programmed with his own memories and brain patterns, could potentially crack, letting the pressure and power get to it, deciding to end everything, quite literally, rather than face an uncaring universe that had no place for him.

Dr. Berger looked at the watch once more. He was filled with an intense realization that he would never take his eyes away from the timepiece now, that it would, indeed, be the last thing he ever saw as it ticked away the final seconds of the grand story of humanity.

10

He choked back a sob. He was not ready. He was not sure anyone ever was.

9

Maybe his calculations were wrong. Maybe he had misread the data surge or somehow the AI had fooled him.

8

No. He was not wrong in this case. He had been wrong to begin this terrible process and his hubris had cost him his soul.

7

Maybe if he admitted that, maybe he would be forgiven in the afterlife, for now, as the seconds ticked away, he fervently hoped there was something waiting for him afterward.

6

Right now he was so terribly alone, as he realized, he had always been. His life was ending the way he had lived it — a solitary man.

5

He would not be afraid. He would not be wracked with guilt. His last seconds would not be filled with those thoughts.

4

He cleared his mind. It was, in the end, all he had left.

3

He breathed deeply. Whatever came next, he was ready.

2

He was a bit surprised. His life was not flashing before his eyes. Time was not slowing down for him. It was merely ticking away.

1

And now it was gone.

Beep…beep…beep…beep. *Beep-beep-beep-beep-beep-beep.*

He closed his eyes and welcomed the end.

ON THE EIGHTH DAY

CHRISTOPHER NADEAU

I hear them outside my window, laughing, screwing, fighting. Animals is what they are. Pure and simple. Stupid, mangy, annoying animals without purpose, without direction.

Without a care.

They are so wrapped up in themselves that they don't even know I'm there, and probably have no idea that someone is living in the house.

As for me, I'm just a tired, useless old man. A non-animal, uninterested in cavorting about, and sticking my dick in whatever wet opening presents itself.

As far as I know, I'm the last civilized human being on the planet.

The sun is barely visible over the horizon, meaning they will soon stop what they're doing and pass out from exhaustion.

Then I'll go outside, armed with two .45 Colt pistols, and blow their damn heads clean off.

At night, this useless old man becomes a one-man cleanup crew.

There's no Adam and Eve here.

The Good Lord does not even gaze down upon this place. Earth, humanity, people, it was all too much of a disappointment to Him.

We didn't even deserve an end-time.

* * *

I was there when God descended from Heaven and spoke to the people of the world. I stood in front of my house and stared up at His majesty, His perfection, and I didn't look away, not even once. I thought he was going to take me with him. Me, and the others who had earned His grace. But instead, he scolded us—all of us—for our lack of vision. He'd had big plans for us, bigger than anything that had been discussed before, and now He was leaving us to our own device.

The atheists were thrilled.

Having been proven wrong about there being no God, they instead were able to say without fear of much contradiction that God didn't give a rat's ass about us. But their giddiness didn't last long.

Most people weren't like me. Most people weren't able to gaze upon God and remain level-headed. Billions of people went insane, overwhelmed by what they'd seen, and heard. In a matter of days, it was as if the logic centers of their brains had shut down.

I watched people get ripped to pieces one after another. Those that weren't eviscerated were used for pleasure in ways even the most demented rapists couldn't have conceived of in the Pre-Revelation days.

It didn't take me long to figure out what needed to be done.

I swung the door wide open, shuddering when it made a loud creaking noise. The remaining sunlight illuminated the inert bodies on the ground, cluttering my front yard. Why do they keep coming here?

In droves, they arrived nightly, as if drawn to me. Ignoring them was impossible. Killing them was a pleasure but I'm old and slow-moving. If I simply stood in my doorway during the day and shot them, it would get me killed, and I'm not ready to go into the Vast Emptiness that now awaits everyone since God walked away.

Without Heaven, nothing awaits me.

The first one was a young female. She was snoring, sleeping against my favorite tree, the one Sara and I'd planted together. She was desecrating my wife's memory by sitting there, one firm breast hanging out of a tattered T-shirt. I raised my arthritic hand with my gun within it and shot her in the heart. I was rewarded with the sound of her gurgling and then exhaling one final breath.

One sinner dispatched, more to come.

My next shots were used on a nude couple entangled on my back porch. Next was a young man sleeping on his side. He looked peaceful, normal. I wanted to believe he'd open his eyes and talk to me like a person. But I won't give him the chance to surprise me. I buried a .45 slug into his brain.

I repeated this pattern as I circled my front yard. I told myself it was like picking weeds out of the ground, from between the cracks in the pavement. After all, are these people not the weeds that ruined the Garden of Eden?

When there was only a couple left to kill, I took a breather, my palm resting against my house as I listened to the *thump-thump-thump* of my heart, the only sound left for me to hear. The only sound I wanted to here.

"Nice work."

I jumped and let out a yell, whirling around, I wrapped my left foot around my right and almost fell. I raised the .45 in my hand at the sudden vocal intrusion, but didn't fire. Standing before me, filthy, hollow-eyed and tiny, was a kid who couldn't be older than fifteen. He was one of those kids who hadn't met puberty in any significant way.

"I'm impressed," he said.

I raised the pistol. "State your purpose."

He put his hands up and smiled. "Easy, General. I'm friend, not foe."

I wanted to trust him but I didn't. It was rare when someone lucid showed up, let alone a kid who should have been too young to learn such good communication skills when the world turned sour.

"I was only admiring your handiwork." The kid swiveled his head from left to right and whistled. "You're like the Orkin man!"

I nodded. "Nice talking to you, son. Time for me to go inside now."

The kid began to pout, actually *pouted*. "Aww, geez. Seriously?"

I stared at him, trying to spot any sarcasm, and decided he was being sincere. "You'd best find a safe place to bed down before the sun comes up."

The kid glanced away, as if embarrassed by my perceived concern. "I'll be all right. Hey, maybe I can stay with you!"

"Forget it." I walked inside and closed the door. By the time I peered through the peephole, there was no sign of him.

The next morning I awoke to the sound of a whole new group of *humanimals* giving in to all their worst instincts and urges. It was as if I'd done nothing the previous night. Why did I even bother? Probably because the only two things I had left were time and bullets.

Something hit my bedroom window hard, and it caused me to stumble out of bed and limp over and look outside. Whatever it was, it was gone by the time I pulled the curtains aside. There was blood all over the glass.

More killing in the name of nothing.

I relieved myself in the bathroom, amazed that the toilet still flushed. I knew the day would come when the plumbing would no longer work. The electricity was already waning, and would sometimes go out to come back on minutes or even hours later. If not for my back-up generator, I wouldn't be able to cook my breakfast each morning on my electric stove with any certainty. At the current rate of consumption and spoilage, I figured Id be long dead before food became a scarcity anyway. The same with fuel for the generator.

While I was eating, a fight broke out on my lawn. It was difficult to understand what was being said but I got the gist of it. It was the same stupid fight that had taken place since time immemorial: Two men, one woman. The yelling continued to escalate until, by the time I'd finished eating, it had become a full-on brawl. At one point, it sounded like someone was knocking on every square inch of my house, one section after another.

This had happened before.

I went into the basement where the noise was muted and tried to do some reading.

I'd grown to like it in my basement. It was more than an escape, it was a sanctuary, the one place that didn't remind me of anything or anywhere else. Superman couldn't have wished for a better hideaway from a demanding world than my basement.

Collapsing on my old vinyl couch with a loud sigh, I spared a glance at the dust-covered Bible on the table next to me. When was the last time I'd opened it? I reached over and picked up my dog-earned copy of *Valis* by Phillip K Dick. The book had never made sense to me before. My wife thought it was brilliant, but it always seemed like a collection of drug-induced meanderings. These days it made too much sense and to an extent that it now frightened me more than what went on outside.

"Good choice. May I also suggest *Towing Jehovah* by James Morrow?"

When I tell you I screamed, I mean I let out a shriek so high-pitched that for a moment I thought a woman had entered the room, I wouldn't be lying. The book flew out of my hand as I struggled to my feet, cursing myself for not having brought a pistol downstairs.

"Didn't mean to frighten you."

I squinted into the darkness behind my reading lamp and saw a small figure standing there, unmoving, arms limp and hands holding nothing dangerous that I could make out.

It was the kid from outside, it had to be.

"How'd you get in here?"

He walked toward me with a sheepish grin. "Wasn't too hard."

I looked away; it was supposed to be impossible. I'd fortified the devil out of this house and the windows were too high off the ground for anyone to reach them, not to mention the bars over them. "What do you want?" I asked.

He looked at me as if I'd just grown an enormous wart in the middle of my face. "In case you haven't been paying attention, it's rather difficult to have a decent conversation these days."

"I'm not really one for excessive talking, son."

The kid chuckled. "Well, anything is better than the nonsense those nuts up there spew."

I'm forced to concede his point and I motioned for him to have a seat. I sat across from him and found myself unable to stop staring. Something about him seemed familiar; although I wasn't sure we'd ever met before. Even stranger, the longer he sat there, the more he seemed like a part of the environment. I was uncomfortable with my level of comfort.

So he stayed that day and we talked, and then I let him stay longer. As the days passed, that feeling of unease was soon forgotten and the kid became a normal part of my daily routine. Pretty soon I couldn't imagine life without him.

The day eventually came when I decided the kid needed to be included in my nightly ritual. To my surprise, he seemed reluctant.

"I could see doing it if they were zombies," he said. "Or, like, werewolves or vampires. But they're still people, right?"

I shrugged. "Barely."

The kid leaned forward from his position sitting on the base-ment couch and frowned in my direction. "What does that mean?"

"It means, kid, my definition of 'people' doesn't include mind-less morons who fuck and kill and sleep where they shit."

"Obviously you didn't have many friends before the Fall." The kid laughed. "You just described half of the planet!"

"This is different, dammit. Something…left when God went away. Some part of them went with Him or something." I sat back and sighed. "Or maybe it just died."

"How come it didn't die in you or me?"

I didn't answer that; how should I know? Were we smarter than the others? Worthier? Luckier? Did it even matter now? As far as I could see, God's absence left a huge hole in the righteous-ness wall. If someone didn't plug it up, none of us would see the future.

"It has to be up to you, I won't force you to help," I said, get-ting to my feet. "It's nearly dark."

The kid didn't join me that night. I could only imagine the look on his face with each report from my gun echoing into the night.

We didn't talk much for a while after that. The kid seemed to be experiencing some growing pains, wrestling with the end of his childhood and the beginning of something much scarier. I sympa-thized. As old as I was, I might not be around much longer to help guide him into adulthood and he knew it.

I didn't invite him outside with me anymore. No point, really, since it was a standing invitation. I couldn't make the kid pick up a gun and kill morons. Besides, it wasn't something I needed help with. They never woke up as they were being shot and killed.

Well, except the day one finally did.

41

The night started out like normal. I walked outside as the sun was setting, gazed about my littered front yard, and me with my two pistols, I started cleansing the world of the truly useless.

It all went as planned until I reached one middle-aged man with a bruised and bloodied face who was snoring so loud it actually overshadowed my .45s when I shot someone nearby him. With a shake of my head, I raised my right gun, aimed between his tightly closed eyes, and then recoiled when those eyes sprung open and he grabbed hold of my left ankle.

My screaming should have woken up all the other sleeping idiots but they didn't so much as stir. I tried to wrench my ankle free, stumbled forward, and landed on my arthritic knee.

"You stop!" the man yelled. "You go! You stop!"

"Make up...your...mind!" I lashed out with the pistol in my right hand, surprised by the sickening sound when it shattered the ranting lunatic's nose.

His hand released its grip on my ankle just enough for me to roll over on my side and aim the weapon at him. My voice came out in a shriek, "Why aren't you sleeping?"

The man covered his nose with both hands and said something unintelligible while rocking back and forth.

"Tell me why you're not sleeping!" I yelled.

He removed his hands from his face and growled like the animal he was. I placed a bullet between his eyes, the top of his head exploding, blood and brain matter splattering the tree behind him.

Now the bastard will sleep whether he wanted to or not.

I told myself it was a fluke. Out of the hundreds of idiots I'd killed, only one had ever woken up while I was doing it. As with anything else, there was bound to be some sort of anomaly. It was nothing to worry about. Besides, the kid didn't seem worried at all.

"Kinda figured that would happen," he said over his breakfast of dry cereal. How's the ankle?"

"Hurts like hell," I said.

The kid nodded and glanced outside by way of the kitchen window. "It's funny. I've seen them all over but they tend to wander around like they have nowhere to go. I've never seen them congregate in one place for so long."

I followed his gaze outside. The kid had a point. It was almost as if... No, that was pure nonsense.

One of them punched a hole through my living room window and peered inside, its forehead striking the metal bars.

"Wow," the kid said. "Intense."

"That's it!" They'd never done this before, never paid me any mind. If they knew I was inside my house, everything was changing. I limped over to the gun cabinet and pulled out my shotgun. "They're finally attacking!"

The kid chuckled. "Nah, I think they're just curious."

I whirled on him, snapping the shotgun into place after sliding in two shells. "They're too stupid to be curious." They're so stupid, in fact, that I was able to walk up to the one peering inside and hit him in the face with the shotgun, right through the bars.

"Ow!" he yelled from outside. "Why hit?"

I gestured toward the window. "Convinced now?"

The kid just smiled, his eyes sad. What was wrong with him? Didn't he get it?

"Grab a gun and follow me," I said.

The kid blinked. "But I don't..."

"Grab the gun or *get out!*"

I didn't wait for his response, already throwing open the door and taking aim at my first idiot, a woman. She flew backwards from the shot, knocking another one to the ground and pinning him there. I cocked the barrels and fired again, this time taking two at once as the bullets passed through one body and into the one behind it.

"They don't seem to be attacking," the kid said from behind me.

I turned to see him holding a .45 limp at his side.

"They will," I said. "Given time, they will."

He raised the pistol and took aim at one standing in the middle of the yard, with his limp genitalia dangling between his legs. The kid said, "Are you really giving me no choice?"

"I gave you a choice, son," I said. "Shoot them or get out. Go it alone."

The kid sighed. He raised his free hand, the one not holding the gun, and made it into a gun shape with his thumb pointed up and his index finger straight out, as if it was the gun barrel, then said, "Bang."

They all fell down, unmoving. All of them, like someone had pressed a button and turned them off.

I exited the doorway and limped over to the nearest one. "I don't...how did...what are you?"

The kid dropped the .45 and smiled kindly. "I see my search continues."

I couldn't keep myself from looking at the unmoving idiots lying on the ground at my feet. Why did I never notice until now how...*perfect* they all looked? Like mannequins given life.

"My God," I whispered.

"If only," the kid said.

I raised the shotgun and leveled it at him. "Who are you?"

"Hope," he said with a shrug. "Curiosity. Desire. Take your pick."

"That doesn't make any sense." I could hear my voice cracking but I didn't care. I was the one with the shotgun.

The kid frowned as if noticing the shotgun for the first time. "You still don't see, do you?" He looked up at the sky. "Perhaps you never will."

It dawned on me that I'd asked the wrong question a moment ago, so I rephrased it. "*What* are you?"

He smiled. "Free Will."

And he was gone, just like that.

In the days that followed, they started coming. People. Real people like me. They were scared to come out, but they've heard about the miracles and they wanted to see them firsthand.

I didn't consider them miracles at all.

Yes, I was able to awaken the idiots on my lawn, and sure, they'd woken up more intelligent than before. And okay, I did the same for all the ones who came to my house after that, but so what? Somebody had to do it, with God gone and all.

But why did it have to be me?

I didn't ask for this. I didn't want it. Now people won't leave me alone. I'm old and tired. Why can't I just die? Except, I don't think I can. Not anymore.

Whatever the kid did to me was permanent. I'm not sure I understood the whole thing, but I think I had to go over the edge before I could return.

Now what?

Is the entire human race my responsibility? Will they build temples in my honor and erect idols to me some day?

Not if I can help it.

This was a second chance, and they better not blow it.

It's said that God created Earth in seven days.

No one ever talked about what happened on the eighth day.

GREEN OF BAD VISIONS

GABINO IGLESIAS

Pestalotiopsis microspora. The name rang a bell. Gabriel tuned out for a second. Dr. Kumar's words became an unintelligible sound in the background, even though the man was speaking only a few feet away from his face. Then it all came back with the speed of rushing water.

He'd read the article about six months before in *Applied and Environmental Microbiology*. Although he recalled the findings, the names of those responsible for the study evaded him. *Pestalotiopsis microspora* was a fungus found in Ecuador by a team of researchers from Yale. The fungus could eat polymer polyester polyurethane via a process called bioremediation. The now nameless researchers had isolated the enzyme that allowed the fungus to break down plastics. If he recalled correctly, the next step would be to mass produce the voracious fungus and then unleash the powers of bioremediation on landfills.

It was the kind of finding that made the news for about three seconds and then disappeared from newspapers and obscure academic journals alike.

Gabriel came back to the conversation just in time to realize he had missed the most crucial part of it.

"…And that's why we need you to start working on this project, Gabriel," Dr. Kumar suggested. "I know how much time you've invested with your research on the Giant Polypore mutation, but I'm asking you to put your time and effort into this as a personal favor. If we don't give the Feds a satisfactory report and convince them that we have this under control, they're going to turn everything over to the Department of Health or the CDC. If they do, those guys will probably waltz in here and put a stop to everything we're working on right now until they can figure out exactly what happened to Dr. Mullen and his son. Considering Mullen was taking work home and that he never brought in any of the samples from his trip to Ecuador, you can bet they'll get on our case about safety measures as well. Do you see how the extent of the repercussions becomes exponentially worse if we don't take care of this now?"

"I understand, sir," Gabriel replied. "I really don't know much about whatever Dr. Mullen was working on." For a man who was more or less completely lost, Gabriel thought he had framed the question in a way that made him seem only curious.

In reply, Dr. Kumar grabbed a yellow folder that was sitting next to his phone and placed it on the desk in front of Gabriel.

"Everything we know is in there," Dr. Kumar nodded at the folder. "We also talked to the police; you'll be granted access into Dr. Mullen's home after tomorrow. They only glanced at his papers so I'm sure they had no idea what they were reading. The detective in charge assured me they didn't remove anything. Apparently, they don't think there was any foul play. They're convinced Mullen breathed in something that affected him on a neurological level, so they only took a cursory look at his home lab and then sealed it off. That means his papers are still there, along with whatever he was working on. I truly hope his notes enlighten you. We need you to put an end to this quickly. If you ask me, I think he was just overworked and his wiring simply short-circuited."

Gabriel wanted to know more. The rumors in the hall were so awful they couldn't be entirely made up, unless whoever started them had an imagination that could give Richard Laymon a run for his money. Those who'd last spoken to him speculated that the man had attempted to gorge himself on a feast of fungi in an attempt to become a plant himself, and in his fit of madness, committed other unspeakable acts upon his son, who'd also perished just as mysteriously. Someone else suggest that Mullen had fancied himself something of a 'prophet,' and he apparently envisioned monstrous fauna consuming overwhelming entire cities.

Doctor Kumar placed a hand on Gabriel's shoulder. "He was a great man, a family man. But now he's dead, along with his son. The rumors must be dispelled. We have a reputation to up-hold…our work is too important for the government to walk in here and shut us down."

Gabriel decided the smart thing to do would be to take the folder and read its contents.

"I'll try my best, Dr. Kumar. Do you think when I'm done I can jump back on the Polypore mutation research? I fear that if we don't figure out how to stop it, the consequences will be disas-trous."

"As soon as you figure out what Dr. Mullen was working on and put together a report that tells the authorities everything's fine, you can go back to saving the trees, Gabriel," Dr. Kumar said with a condescending smile and a nod. Gabriel knew the nod well—it meant the conversation was over.

Gabriel looked at the man sitting across from him and won-dered how long it would take him to satisfy his boss. He wanted to flip through the folder, but there would be time for that later. Instead of looking at it, Gabriel used the folder to wave his good-bye. A second later, he was out of the chair and exiting Dr. Kumar's office into the brightly-lit hallway.

Up ahead, the door to his lab stood open. He belonged in his lab, working on a strange mutation of the Giant Polypore fungus.

Known scientifically as *Meripilus giganteus*, the Giant Polypore fungus had long been the nemesis to Beech trees. Once the fungus latched on to the root of a tree, rot would quickly follow. This turned affected trees into dangerous giants that could fall on someone with the help of single gust of wind.

In the last year, *Meripilus giganteus* had mutated.

A ranch owner in Montana had seen four Ponderosa Pines come crashing down on his property in the same week. The man's wife happened to be a professor in the College of Agriculture at Montana State University. She made a few calls and the problem had landed in Gabriel's lap. The fact that he had a PhD in Plant Pathology from Cornell made Dr. Kumar throw anything that had to do with plants his way.

Gabriel sat at his desk and opened the folder. He craved coffee, but his curiosity about Dr. Mullen's death was more powerful than his need for caffeine.

The first few pages were Dr. Raphael Mullen's vita. Its thickness was impressive. The folder also contained printed articles and interviews with the doctor, who was undoubtedly one of the top microbiologists of his generation. It was all stuff Gabriel had read or heard about before.

The last page was a note from the police. It stated that no further information could be provided about the ongoing investigation regarding the death of Dr. Raphael Mullen. The note also made it clear that Dawson Research, the company Gabriel worked for, was welcome to send one of its own to look into the deceased doctor's home lab. There was a small card with a scribbled cell phone number. Underneath it, a name scrawled in the same tight cursive: Paul Monroe. Gabriel would have to call that man to set up a time for them to meet. The detective would grant him access to Mullen's home and lab.

He decided to get that cup of coffee and take care of the call after.

The sun was high and there were no clouds in the sky when Gabriel parked on the curb in front of Mullen's home. The front of the house was split in half by a big chimney and decorative half-timbering, which gave the two-floor Tudor a look that danced between medieval and creepy.

A man that Gabriel took to be Paul Monroe stood by the door, even though their meeting was not scheduled for another ten minutes. Gabriel got out of the car, locked it, and approached the man.

Monroe had an angular face with a five o'clock shadow and a receding hairline. He was wearing a blue polo shirt that was a bit tight across his muscular chest, shoulders, and arms. Gabriel said hello to the detective and stuck his hand out. Monroe took the proffered hand and gave it a few hard, slow shakes.

"You Gabriel?" asked Monroe in a deep, powerful voice.

"Yes, sir. Detective Monroe, right?"

"Call me Paul."

Letting go of Gabriel's hand, Monroe turned toward the door and pulled a set of keys out of his front pocket.

"Everyone who had to be in here has already come and gone, and that's why we gave you guys access. We know about Muller's recent trip to Ecuador and a lot of people would breathe easier if we knew that he simply went of his trolley. People don't want to believe that he brought something back from his trip that could kill both him and his son. Were you familiar with his work?"

The detective had opened the door while he spoke. Both men were now standing in Mullen's living room. The scant furniture and lack of decorations on the walls confirmed what Gabriel had already supposed: Raphael Mullen had been a man for whom work always came first. Divorced almost as soon as his son was born, Mullen had basically done nothing but work for most of his life.

"Mullen was a microbiologist," Gabriel pointed out. "He became obsessed with the properties of *Pestalotiopsis microspora*, a fungus that can eat plastic. He took a trip to Ecuador when his latest discoveries were released to the public. He spent a few weeks with the *Huaorani*, a group of semi-nomadic Indians who live in the Amazon rain forest. Mullen thought the tribe's shamans were natural experts in all things horticultural. My guess is that he was interested to see how some of these fungi interact with other microorganisms in different scenarios."

Although Gabriel was only replying to the detective's question, he could tell by the look on Monroe's face that his interest had waned. The man had probably expected something darker when it came to what Mullen did with his life and the reasons for his trip.

Monroe asked, "Do you think there's even a slight possibility that something he brought back from the rain forest could've made him crazy?"

The question took Gabriel by surprise. He'd spent hours of his time delving into the wild rumors and theories regarding Mullen's death, but he still didn't know exactly how Mullen had died. Within his social circles, the reputable doctor had become something of an eccentric. Those who spoke with him before his mysterious death mentioned that Mullen would often ramble about 'apocalyptic' scenarios featuring an invincible, indomitable fungi.

"To be honest, I might be able to answer your question if I knew a bit more about how he died. The file I was given contained no details whatsoever."

Monroe looked at him for a long, tense moment before replying.

"That information hasn't been given out to anyone. The media would have a party if we gave them the gruesome details. If I tell you and then something leaks out to the press, I know who to look for. Am I making myself clear?"

The threat was not lost on Gabriel. Since he had no plans to talk to any reporters—and anything Monroe told him could possibly help him write the report sooner—he assured the detective the information was safe with him. His business, Gabriel explained, was with whatever was in Mullen's lab.

"Dr. Raphael Mullen was apparently upstairs in his lab with his son, Scott Mullen," Monroe explained. "We can only assume he was showing his kid something he found interesting. According to the mother, the teenager spent odd weekends with his father and shared an interest for his work. As far as we know, Mullen came at him from behind at some point and stabbed him three times in the neck using a pen. With his son bleeding to death on the floor, Mullen tried to start a fire in the trash bin. At some point, he used the same pen he'd killed his son with to gouge his own eyes out and then stab himself in the carotid artery. He bled to death blind, probably thinking his fire was a success. Since there was very little paper in the bin, the fire puttered out. The cleaning lady found both bodies the following morning."

The image of Dr. Mullen stabbing himself in the neck with a pen after gouging out his own eyes made Gabriel feel a tad woozy. Not one word of what Monroe said made any sense.

"I...nothing he brought back from the rain forest could've possibly made him commit such... horrible acts."

"That's good to know," Monroe nodded. "I'm ready to read a report by you guys saying it's all clear so we can send a cleaning team in here and close this case once and for all. However, you have to understand that we're a little worried. We're talking about a respectable, educated man here. Something had to be terribly wrong with him for him to kill his own kid, you know? We usually don't run into murder-suicides where the perpetrator maims himself before committing suicide. We've interviewed everyone who could give us information about Mullen and they were all just as surprised as you are. Mullen wasn't the type of person who would do something like this. The fact that it all went down in his lab makes us really worried about the possibility that there might be something in there capable of affecting people in a similar way."

A low buzz reached Gabriel's ears. Monroe pulled a cell phone out of his back pocket and flipped it open. A few monosyllabic answers later, the detective clapped the phone shut and looked at him.

"I have to get out of here," Monroe said while handing Gabriel the bundle of keys. "When you're done, either drop these at the station or give me a call. If I'm nearby, I'll drop by and pick them up."

Gabriel grabbed the keys and thanked the detective.

"No problem. I hope you can find something that helps us put this thing to rest. Best of luck up there."

Without another word, the detective turned around and walked out the door. Gabriel followed him. While the detective drove away, Gabriel opened his car trunk and picked up the box of gloves and the disposable face mask he brought from home.

Although the sun was still as bright as when Gabriel had arrived just a few minutes before, an icy pair of fingers ran down his back as he turned to look at the empty house behind him. As he walked to the door again, the image of Dr. Mullen driving an already bloodied pen through his neck came back to him. The icy hand ran back up Gabriel's back and wrapped itself around the nape of his neck.

Monroe had said nothing about which key opened the lab, so it took Gabriel a good deal of time trying until he figured out which one did the trick. As for the lab itself, it had been very easy to spot. As soon as he reached the second floor, Gabriel saw the door at the very end of the hallway crisscrossed with yellow tape that read, "POLICE LINE DO NOT CROSS." He placed his gloves and mask on the floor and fumbled with his keys. He used one of the keys to cut through the tape and felt somewhat guilty about it, even though he'd been granted permission to enter the room.

The sight on the other side of the lab's door was something no one could have prepared him for. Within the massive room there were three stainless steel lab tables pushed against the left wall. To the right, a large metal desk with a Formica top that seemed to have been pulled from a government office from the '70s held a microscope and some folders. Along the back wall, three wall cabinets that were stacked on top of each other and a fridge completed the lab. All three tables, the entire wall behind them, and about half of the floor were covered in dark green fungi. Whatever Mullen had been working on was now covered in something that looked like green mold gone wild.

Considering Mullen's death had only taken place six days before and that the team of investigators had been there for two days, the mess Gabriel was looking at had happened in just under four days. That rate of growth was impossible. He walked over to the desk and took a seat. He didn't have to rummage around too much to find what he was looking for. Mullen was a very organized man and the only two folders on his desk had to do with his most current research.

Gabriel opened the first folder and started reading the first sheet. He was surprised to see it was written in Spanish. He never knew Mullen spoke a second language. As Gabriel read more, he learned that Mullen spoke the Huaorani language and a bit of Qechua as well. The notes seemed to be Spanish translations of conversations Mullen had sustained with the Huaorani people and other folks he met during his travels in Ecuador.

While looking for *Pestalotiopsis microspora*, Mullen had run into a very different fungus. When he asked a Huaorani shaman about it, Mullen learned the natives avoided the green fungi at all costs and called it 'Green of Bad Visions' in their native tongue. The shaman explained that those who listened to the music of the Green of Bad Visions were bound to go crazy and take their own life. The fungus was considered an evil spirit and the Huaorani refused to camp in places where fungi could be found growing within a short distance.

According to the notes, touching the Green of Bad Visions caused people to have horrible hallucinations. Tribe members who touched it were always found dead or blabbering about the end of the world.

Gabriel read through the rest of the first folder. It was mostly translated conversations from the trip, theories about how the

Pestalotiopsis microspora had developed an enzyme that could process chemicals that weren't naturally found in its habitat, and some observations about how the *Huaorani* produced some of the most plague-resistant manioc in the world by constantly changing the soil in which they planted and stayed away from monocultures.

The notes were interesting, but there wasn't anything that served Gabriel's purpose. The second folder turned out to have exactly what he was looking for.

Mullen had subjected his samples to a plethora of tests and he'd recorded the way the fungi reacted. Gabriel pulled out a sheet and read it.

Mullen had either lost his mind, or it was the strangest fungus in the world.

The samples showed no reaction whatsoever to water or heat, something that was unheard of. Likewise, the samples ate through organic and non-organic matter at the same alarming rate. On the third day, Mullen had walked into the lab to find that the fungi had eaten through their respective Petri dishes and were beginning to corrode the stainless steel table. That meant the fungi were somehow chloridic in nature, which was also unheard of.

Not willing to trust the notes of a man who killed his son and then plucked out his own eyes, Gabriel got up and walked over to the fungi-covered table. As he approached, a low hum stopped him in his tracks. At first he thought the sound was coming from the fridge, but upon turning his head, he realized it was coming from the table. He took another step. The hum grew louder. He looked at the table and thought he saw movement. It looked as if a small snake had moved underneath the blanket of green fungi which covered the first table.

His mind was obviously playing tricks on him. Gabriel walked back and sat down. He picked up the notes and started going over them again. The more he read, the crazier Mullen's claims became. The microbiologist wrote he thought the fungi on his tables were making music. After a few more lines, the writing became incoherent babble.

"I touched the samples," read the page in Gabriel's hand. "Something happened and I woke up to Scott shaking me. Wanted to know if there was anything left of the Petri dishes. Now it's inside me. Watched it sink into Scott's hand as well. I've seen what's to come. I don't want us to be here when it happens. The shaman was right."

Like someone waking from a deep sleep inside an airplane and noticing the sound of the engines for the first time, Gabriel noticed the hum was gone, replaced by a low sound that alternated its pitch slightly. He focused on the sound. It wasn't music, but there was definitely a rhythm to it. As a plant pathologist, Gabriel knew some plants were capable of amazing things, but emitting a rhythmic sound was completely new to him. Maybe finding something so incredible had driven Mullen crazy.

Leaving the notes behind, Gabriel walked back to the tables. This time, he kept on walking even when the sound became louder at his approach. Now there appeared to be multiple snakes moving under the green blanket. He thought about the gloves, but he had left them outside the door when he was cutting the police tape. Before he could catch himself, Gabriel reached out and ran his finger across the green blanket of fungi. It felt incredibly cold. Then a shock rocked his body and forced him to close his eyes.

The first sensation was strange, as if someone was trying to stretch his skull. The sound coming from the fungi became an unbearable cacophony of screams and unintelligible blabber. A bright flash of light momentarily blinded him. When he opened his eyes, a tepid, airless heat sucked the breath from his lungs. Ancient trees loomed over him, their thick canopy obscuring the sun's light. He could smell the moist earth beneath his feet as the screams and blabber subsided to the chattering of a million creatures.

Was he dreaming or somehow unconscious? While Gabriel spun around in a wide circle, his eyes quickly identifying and cataloging familiar vegetation patterns, he understood where he was, though he couldn't believe it to be possible.

He was surrounded by the dense vegetation of the Amazon rain forest.

Gabriel's scientific mind struggled with his horrifying predicament. How was such a thing possible? In all of his scientific inquiries, no man had ever discovered the ability to instantaneously transport his body to another part of the world. While he struggled with his newfound reality, he searched the sky for any light that might be able to penetrate that dark, forest floor.

Then, he watched as a nude boy-child approach over the twisted, chaotic brambles. Gabriel wanted to say something, but he knew that the child wouldn't be able to understand him. The boy stopped and opened his mouth to the canopy above. With arching fingers, the boy slowly reached for the exposed flesh on his neck.

Gabriel opened his own mouth—a rush of warm air escaped through his throat. A painful chill tightened every muscle in his body; he was immobile, trapped by the invisible prowess of all-encompassing fear.

Nothing made sense, and he believed deep down that the boy's life was in danger. His shirt stuck to his body while blood boiled against the walls of his head. The boy's fingers clawed savagely at his own neck, releasing thick rivulets of scarlet that raced down the length of his hairless chest. The boy clawed, and clawed, and clawed, his wide mouth open in a scream that wouldn't come.

The bright flash of light once again assaulted Gabriel's senses, and he found himself back in the lab. Dr. Mullen's body lay on the floor. There were ragged, dark holes where his eyes were supposed to be.

Before Gabriel could react, the blinding white light pulsed again.

His perspective changed to that of someone looking up from the floor. Two hooded figures were standing over him. Their faces were dark and reptilian in nature. The same cold, inescapable fear held him hostage as he stared up at those monstrous visages. Large black eyes reflected his own shaking face; he stared at his own reflection in those bulbous, abyssal orbs and watched sweat streak along his face. His bladder loosened and warm urine pooled beneath him.

While Gabriel found himself enslaved by those terrifying black eyes, the two creatures merely stood over him, watching him from within the shadows of their hoods. His thoughts raced uncontrollably until a brief moment of icy calm gave him pause, a moment of still peace that eased his labored breathing. His mind had somehow collected itself, as he seemed to come to a final resolution…this surreal experience had corrupted Dr. Mullen, and thus, Gabriel was another victim of this vile, unspeakable power.

Behind the hooded creatures that stood over him, the outline of two monolithic structures rose into a heavy gray fog.

The white light flashed again and he opened his eyes.

The floor felt cold against his cheek. He hesitated for a moment—he was alive. His sweat-moistened shirt and urine-soaked jeans were little consolation for surviving a moment in the throes of madness.

When he raised himself up, Gabriel realized he had been lying on top of the fungi. A painful frost crept up his hands and locked his elbows in place. His arms felt incredibly heavy as he lifted them up to his face; a thick green sludge was penetrating his flesh. With his eyes wide open and frozen, he watched as the last of the green fluid disappeared within the pores along his forearms, as if his body had devoured the green substance. The same inhuman voices he'd heard when he first appeared in the Amazon once again tormented him, though the volume and intensity of the mad concert had grown in strength.

He lowered his hands and stood up. His feet felt rubbery as he took his first step. Something was wrong with his legs. Gabriel bent down to touch his ankles and saw his hands and forearms. Green spots blanketed his skin and a bulbous growth pulsated near his left thumb.

He was infected with something he didn't understand, and as a man of science, his terror overpowered any sense of wonder he might feel.

Deep within his heart, he knew the visions he had been shown accurately depicted fractions of the past as well as the future. He had to call Monroe and let him know what was happening. Mullen had the right idea before he died: burn the house to the ground.

He looked around in search of something he could use to start a fire. The green fungi now covered almost every surface of the room. The hum reached his ears and muddled his thoughts. *Fire*, he thought again. The kitchen was his only option. Stumbling around on wobbly legs, Gabriel made his way downstairs.

Mullen owned an electric stove. Gabriel knew there had to be at least some matches in one of the drawers. When he reached for the first drawer, he noticed the tips of his fingers had flattened considerably and were becoming rounded. The skin on his arms was now mostly green. The strange voices in his head were becoming louder and his right leg twitched as if independent from his body. He pulled the drawer open. It contained only cutlery. A sudden movement came again. His leg was apparently trying to move on its own. Gabriel reached down to pull his pant leg up and the leg jerked back by itself, forcing him to topple forward and bump his head against a cabinet door.

There was some feeling remaining in his left leg and both his arms, but it was quickly disappearing as the blabbering and humming inside his skull maintained its steady crescendo. Then the research came back on its own, breaking through Gabriel's fear and desperation and stunning him into momentary inaction with its implications.

Ophiocordyceps unilateralis. It had been found in the Zona da Mata area in south-eastern Brazil a few months before *Pestalotiopsis microspora*. Scientists had discovered an entire family of fungi that could control ants by releasing chemicals into their brain. The ants became infected by coming into contact with spores. Once infected, they would leave the nest, bite into a leaf and die in that position. The fungus inside each ant would then sprout a spore-bearing stalk out of the back of the neck of the dead ant and release its spores.

This was the fungus that had delivered a horrible fate unto Doctor Mullen. The Huaorani, all along, had the infectious *Ophio-cordyceps unilateralis*. What would happen to the rest of the world if this fungus escaped the sanctity of the lab? If ants could be reduced to such a savage state...what would happen to people?

Gabriel knew he was experiencing something similar to what the ants had been victim to. This fungi, however, acted much faster and was obviously only the beginning of a bigger, more intelligent life form.

Suddenly, both his legs carried him toward the door. Gabriel understood the same thing Mullen had.

Mullen had touched the fungi and became infected. So had his son, Scott. If Gabriel allowed this thing to fully take control of his body and walk out of the house, his death would only be the beginning of the end.

He tried to reach for his cell phone to call Monroe, but his right arm remained dangling uselessly by his side. Whatever was inside him was acting quickly.

All the scientific knowledge packed inside his brain told Gabriel there was only one way to get rid of such a deadly parasite.

What about all of the other dangerous fungi, including the tree-eating *Meripilus giganteus*, the very fungus that was the subject of Gabriel's own studies?

The entire world would be in the grip of an unstoppable power: the combined strength of nature's terrible secrets coming to bear upon the unsuspecting human race.

Gabriel had to prevent that from happening.

Without another thought, the plant pathologist used his left hand to reach into the drawer in front of him. The knife had a serrated edge.

Gabriel heard his flesh rip open as he dragged the utensil across his neck. There was no pain. His hands were already consumed by the parasite, so he didn't bring them up to stop the blood that was spraying out of him.

In the back of his mind, even over the cacophony of inhuman voices, Gabriel knew that was a good thing. Then, the voices began to ebb away as the kitchen around him became dimmer.

Finally, like a light breaking through a cloudy sky, one last thought beamed into his brain: he hadn't found the damn matches.

SMOTHERED

DANA BELL

Funny how all the stories you read about the world endin' always says it goes out with a bang or a whimper or all sudden-like and unexpected. The people weren't prepared for what happened and oh, how awful!

Truth is—that's not what happened at all. The world got smothered and we knew it was comin'.

Yep, you heard right. No earthquakes, no super volcanoes, no explodin' sun, no ice age, no whatever them movie makers used to come up with to make lots and lots of money in movie theaters that don't exist any more.

We got smothered. Plain and simple.

How'd it happen you ask? Well, you remember all that borin' history stuff the teachers forced you to read about in school? That's how it happened—again. Only, it weren't confined to one area of the world. No siree.

It started in the plain states just like before. History says it was only durin' the 1930's but don't you believe it. I found a reference in some old book to it havin' happened fifty years before. Convenient though, how folks just forget about stuff and if it didn't happen in their life time, well, it was like a shiny new toy.

Anyway, there was this drought. Now, in and of itself that's not unusual. It happens that a lot of folks only notice it more because of the cities and them havin' to let the grass get all dried out and crinkly yellow. Not to mention weather people who were always tryin' to forecast whether it'll rain or snow or be so hot you could roast a chicken on your car hood. Like they have a clue what the Lord Almighty had ordained for the day.

So it got all dry and the farmers started worryin' about their crops and the stock market hit a low like they'd never seen for, oh, I don't know, the last time it collapsed. Prices climbed in the stores and before you knew it everyone was screamin' for the government to do somethin'. Not that Congress are worth more than a good milkin' cow or a goat, if you believe they're worth anythin' at all.

They tried, Lord bless 'em. Didn't help. Prices kept jumpin' up almost every day. Good hard workin' folk couldn't afford to feed their families and just when every one thought it couldn't get any worse, yep, you guessed it. It did.

First sign we got was the huge tornado sweepin' down out of the black billowin' clouds and snappin' up every farm and town in its path. Tore up a ten mile radius path from sunny Texas to almost the Canadian border. The accompanying hail pounded all the fields of wheat, barley and other crops down to broken mushy weeds.

Storm chasers called it a freak of nature and measured it as a category 7, although I've heard some say it was actually a ten. They downgraded 'cause some Senator didn't want needless panic. Like folks weren't panicked already.

The old windin' gal herself, the Missip, spilled her banks and washed away more farms and towns. My, my, my, what a mess and couldn't we have more Federal aid on account we need a hand out. Not that it really helped. Most lost all they had and ended up livin' in them shanty towns that began croppin' up 'cuz the bankers, stingy old, you know whats, in cahoots with the buildin' guys, wouldn't put in housin' that decent folks could buy. Just catered to the rich like they were the most important.

Now I'm sure you're wonderin' why I'm a talkin' about all this. I'm just settin' the scene as them movie guys do before all hell breaks loose.

Next came the spiders. Don't imagine you remember that Big honkin' Black Widows who killed more children than any famine or plague since. Built their webs in the corners of houses and snuck up on the youngun's while they slept. Parents didn't know what happened, and before they could get 'em to the nearest hospital, well, I doubt I really have to spell it out for you.

The spiders were followed by the centipedes and the locusts and the grasshoppers. Darned varmints ate just about anythin' that was left and I heard stories of some folks eatin' tumbleweeds. Bitter tastin' stuff. Wasn't bad with a bit of salt though if you didn't mind pickin' bugs out.

Then one day some big city news reporter took his camera crew out to show all the damage that had been done on the farms. While they were shootin' footage, a violent wind came up. What a sight that was. Them tryin' keep them huge cameras perched on their shoulders like the trained hawks you used to see at those fancy fairs or at the national parks, when they were still open for all to visit.

I still remember visitin' Yellowstone and watchin' them geysers spew boilin' hot water everywhere. And those stinky mud pots. Blub, blub. Smelled like sulfur, you know, like the chem stuff in them useless classes you no longer need. Not today anyhow. And the critters, well, they didn't seem to mind. They were everywhere. Buffalo, coyotes, wolves, eagles and…

Sorry, what did you say? What does that have to do with the wind? Nothin'. Nothin' at all. 'Fraid at my age, my mind tends to wander a bit.

Speakin' of which, did you hear about old man Crowder down the way? Seems his kids finally had to lock him in his bedroom. Seems he kept wanderin' off and lookin' for his dog. Problem is, he ain't had a dog for at least twenty some odd years. The old hound got stuck in the swamp. Yeah, I know, there ain't no swamp no more. But he got himself bit by a water moccasin. It's a snake, you see. A poisonous one. No, they ain't down here. Died off so I heard.

Big old snakes though, they still be around. Like to slither into the chicken coop and stir up the hens and steal the eggs and sometimes a young chick. I killed one the other day. Cut off his round head with a shovel I did. Still remember the shocked look in his tiny button eyes, like he had a brain or somethin'.

I had a granddaughter once who almost stepped on one. She went to a concert in Mountainview. Oh, you remember the place; they used to have a type of country fair there. At night they'd have a concert featurin' that good old music you don't hear no more. Lucky for her, her boyfriend was with her and kept her from gettin' bit. They ain't dangerous but there's always the danger of infection.

Heard she moved up north before the smotherin' started, where it ain't so bad like it is here. Seems the mountains in Alaska block the wind some but beware the valleys. They get dumped on. Dust so deep you could drown in it if you dared to try and cross it.

Seems strange not to have to worry about drownin' in water no more. The rivers are all mud now, oozin' down their paths and pourin' into the ocean. Heard the other day it won't be long till there are no more oceans, or fish or whales or any swimming critter God put on this Earth since before man walked upon it.

We got no one to blame but ourselves. Or maybe, like those who believe in Gaia say, the planet just plain got tired of us.

That's why the wind came and the dust. It started in the plain states like before, even reached the East and buried D.C., N.Y. and Boston. It stopped the subways and I have to laugh at that. Buried folks underground or so I heard, and knocked down them high and mighty skyscrapers. The Empire State Building ain't no more. Its spire nose got clipped and killed folks in the streets. Rest of it came crashin' down and crushed the taxis and whoever was walkin' around.

Tragedy it was. Horrible. I prayed for their lost souls. I ain't seen worse since the Twin Towers got blown up—no wait that was my father who saw that. I remember him tellin' me about it and how he cried as he watched people die by jumpin' out the windows. The fire on the upper levels must have been God-awful.

But it wasn't as God-awful as what happened to us. That wind and dust just kept goin'. It didn't stop at our borders. It crossed into Canada, Mexico, and even farther south.

They all saw it comin', but no one left their homes. No one, not even the government, tried to do anythin'. I mean, it ain't like they could have done anythin' anyway.

I still recall the day it finally crossed the Atlantic and hit England, France and them European countries. They all blamed it on us and called us all sorts of names and said we were young upstarts and how we ruined everythin' for everyone else.

Fools. It wasn't our fault. The dust from their fields joined ours and just journeyed on to Asia, China, India. Funny thing is, there was this dust storm over in the, oh, what was the name of that desert? Ah, well, don't matter. It joined the dust storm too, crossin' over the Koreas and Japan, and even fallin' on the islands all over the Pacific.

Eventually, it made it back to the western coast and I remember the panic and fear hittin' and the Hollywood sign crackin' and bein' torn off the mountain.

That's when the movies stopped bein' made. We ain't had one here for, oh, since I was a teenager, I think. Miss 'em I do. All the action and things blowin' up and car chases.

That's why I'm thankful for books. They're harder to destroy. Least I have somethin' to read now and again. When my eyes ain't too tired, although I probably need glasses. Just too bad they can't be found no more. Yeah, I mean both the books and the glasses. Publishers all gone now. Internet too mostly. Sometimes I hear from somebody elsewhere but not so much as in the early days.

Radio waves and TV signals can't get through the dust. It's so thick you don't dare go outside. You'd choke in an instant. There's no sunlight. The trees and plants and stuff have all been stripped down to the roots and even those I expect have died.

Animals have been long gone except the few we managed to get down here underground. Mostly the service ones, like cows, pigs, chickens, and the like. There's even a dog or two and I thought I saw a cat the other day. Glad to see it. I hate rats; them varmints seem to survive no matter what, along with the snakes and a couple of rattlers.

Luckily, most of them are confined down in the older areas of the mine. Yep, you heard me right, a mine. I've been here in an old salt quarry in the middle of what was once Kansas. My family managed to get here, and were among the fortunate few who got chosen. There was a lottery you see. There were many lotteries.

Here in Kansas. In the Carlsbad Caverns in New Mexico, the many in South Dakota, Blanchard Cave in Arkansas, anywhere there was a cave or mine big enough for folks to live in.

They're nice, once you get used to not seein' the sun or walkin' on grass. The temperature's comfy and the dust don't get down here.

We pushed hydroponics to be developed. Had a few years where there weren't enough to eat, but most of us survived that.

There are other health issues, like our bones bein' brittle or our eyes not likin' the light. Still, folks adjusted. I know I have. I feel like a cave bat sometimes. Speakin' of which, they're real good eatin'.

Only real problem we have is the elevator. The dust seeps into the joints and gears and there's a fear we might never be able to escape our dark dungeon.

But it's not like we have any real reason to go back to the surface, anyways. It's dead now and that was so long ago I sometimes have problems rememberin' what it was like.

What did the sun feel like on my face? My toes itch to wiggle in green spiky grass. How did the rain smell after a spring shower? And I long to hear the crickets sing.

I think I saw fireflies once, flickerin' over a field of tall grass. Sparklin' and snappin' in the darkness, like Fourth of July fireworks, only my neck didn't get a crick from trying to watch 'em.

Yeah, I know, my mind is wanderin' again. It does that the older I get. But I try to share what it was once like above ground and how it all came to be.

We need to remember.

Our children need to and theirs and theirs after that and until such a time as we can escape this old salt mine.

If we ever can. I hold the hope we can. One day. Lord willin'.

Until then, remember this one thing, children. Our world didn't die like them rare movies you get to see when the old projector agrees to work.

There were no earthquakes and the sun didn't go nova or an ice age didn't creep down from the north. Instead, it all came with dust and wind.

The planet got smothered.

Like the way you smother taters with cheese. Yummm. It's one of my favorite breakfast foods. And sometimes I eat it for lunch or for dinner. There's no bad time for 'em.

And taters, they grow real good down here.

GOOD NIGHT, B

RONALD O. BORAS

The world is not ending with a bang or even a whimper but—to my eternal disappointment—with a collection of clichés.

I suppose that I, with my quest to find my true love before I'm swallowed whole by the raging earth, am a cliché myself but, then again, I've never claimed to be original. And, really, who among us can make that claim?

In every culture on the planet, creation stories are filled with wild tales of imagery. Now, of course, we'll never know for sure if the universe was created from an enormous explosion of energy and matter, a cow licking the surface of an icy cave, or any of a million other theories of existence passed down through the ages. We've run out of time in our search for the truth.

We won't know the secrets of creation, but what I've come to realize now, unfortunately, is that the end of the world is no Ragnarok or battle of the gods. It is, instead, it's just a sad group of humans facing down the destruction of their world with tears, blood and piles of debris.

Years ago—before the world broke—my friends would play a game. In a light moment, they'd ask, "If this was your last day on earth, what would you do?" Most people, hewing to the spirit of the game, would spin tales of great deeds left undone, perhaps imagining they would travel to distant lands or paint beautiful portraits or spend the day making love to their mates.

I, on the other hand, always took a more pragmatic approach to the query. After all, I reasoned, if I was facing my final day, I imagined I would spend it weeping, gnashing my teeth, beating my chest and cursing the fates, regretting every wasted moment, every missed opportunity and ruing the fact that I would have no more second chances, no more tomorrows to make amends.

Though an honest answer it was, I suppose, a bit of a downer, and my friends always chastised me for giving it. Turns out, I was more prescient than anyone imagined.

Over the decades, there have been plenty of tales — movies, novels, and collections of short stories — about the end of the world. Since the Cold War, I suppose, it has been a topic that preyed on the mind of creative people. Still, in those movies and books, the characters always seemed to act logically and rationally, whether they were contemplating suicide via poison pill or spending time walking along the beach or any of a number of other, equally wise and thoughtful activities.

Well, in the real world, it didn't quite work like that. There was a lot less wisdom and a lot more panicking and rioting, blood and wreckage.

Part of that chaos can be pinned on the actions of our government, of course. They could have handled matters a lot differently, a lot better. They could have told us the truth, for one thing. Or they could have given us more warning. When the earth started rumbling and breaking apart and oozing fiery rage and devouring people and buses and skyscrapers, well, by then, it was too late to quell the panic, wasn't it? I can't really blame the public for freaking out a bit, now can I?

Not me, though. I was, to my utter surprise, completely unfazed.

While the rest of the world was panicking, running amok, smashing windows, grabbing loot, shooting and stabbing, raping and killing — themselves and others, well, I had a moment of clarity.

The moment the world started to fall apart at the seams, I began walking.

I was lucky, in a lot of ways. I made it out of my home state of CT and past New York before the first big Cratering Event (as they've come to be called) occurred, when the Atlantic Ocean swallowed most of the northeast, and I was already deep into New Jersey when the government — or what was left of it, declared martial law. As I walked, day in and day out, night after night, I managed to evade the fighting between the soldiers and the people they were meant to protect.

Plus, I was fortunate enough to avoid the smaller Cratering Events: the cracking earth, the toppling buildings and the lava spurts. Well, if fortunate is a word that still exists in this cold, worn world. After all, anyone remaining, who, like me, can avoid both the symptomatic death rattle of the planet and the animalistic rage of its forsaken creatures, well, we both have a front row seat for the end of everything, with nary a space-bound ark in sight. I wouldn't say we hang much on fortune.

But, even in the final hours of the world, I knew I was fortunate. I had a purpose in my life, or what remained of it. I wasn't just walking for my health (after all, with all of our days numbered in single digits, perhaps, the desire to focus on healthy pursuits had disintegrated like the final vestiges of civilized behavior). I had, in my heart at least, a goal. It was, perhaps, a foolish pursuit, but it gave me a reason to go on and, in these final days, that was something most people sadly lacked.

I was going to find her if it was the last thing I did. And, of course, it would be.

I just had to hope that she was headed for the same place as I was. And these days, all I had left, like the bottom of Pandora's Box after the unleashing of the world's evil, was hope.

My hope had existed, in varying strengths, for quite a long time now. Perhaps it just seemed like a lifetime because, when the rest of your existence can be calculated in hours using simple arithmetic, time measured in years or decades seems to stretch on forever. But, in reality, it was barely more than a decade and a half.

Sixteen years BA—Before the Apocalypse, as I had started to count time—I met Linda. Back then, when we were young and stupid, we imagined we had our whole lives ahead of us. Nowadays, with the end of everything so near, it was hard to believe we were ever that naïve. Though, since we were in Washington, DC when we met, I suppose you could make the case that we were surrounded by the seeds of The End, that the decisions made in marbled hallways only miles from our bourgeoning relationship would lead the world to this moment, this grand end of all things.

But of course, we couldn't have anticipated any of this when our lives first touched. The end of the world was the last thing on our minds when we sat down in that creative writing class our senior year. And, when she asked me to be her partner on the dialogue project, the possibilities had seemed endless.

But, as I traversed the Garden State, watching the world crumble around me, I realized that the endless possibilities had collapsed down to a single, unavoidable destiny.

The walking was not easy, I'll tell you that much. I had never been one to keep in shape. There would always be time for that, I thought. Well, that was not entirely true. There had been one time, a couple years ago, when my physical shape had been the highest of priorities, when I had the idea to sculpt my scrawny, doughy frame into something that might be appealing to a member of the opposite sex (well, one member in particular). And, of course, in the back of my mind, I had the notion that, if I had an opportunity to impress this woman, a physically fit body could come in handy in other arenas. I mean sexually, of course.

I could have phrased that in a classier fashion, but I figure, if the world's going to end, if I can't be banging chicks myself, I can at least think about the act.

There was a price my body had to pay as I walked, mile after mile, hour after hour, day after day. But, even as my health began to fail me, there was a payoff. As society crumbled, obtaining valuable items—anything I needed, really—was easier than ever.

I had to change my shoes more frequently than I'd have thought, but it was simple enough to find replacements. The first time I scavenged a pair off of a fresh corpse, it made my soul shiver. But the second time, it was much easier. Eventually, I didn't even care if the body was decayed or not. Issues of fit and comfort were far more important than odor. After all, I walked all day and never bathed, so I smelled as ripe as any stinking corpse.

The scavenging became easier as I traversed the ruins of America. I took food when I wanted to, changed clothes when I felt like it and, after witnessing a particularly brutal slaughter of a group of travelers somewhere outside of Teaneck, I armed myself.

Of course, Linda had been the true weapon's expert. She'd told me, during our year of passionate e-mails, the she had learned to shoot after she'd escaped a rather unpleasant situation on the Brooklyn subway late one night. She'd promised to teach me to use a weapon when we finally reunited. But that, of course, had not happened, as our little world had crumbled long before the rest of humanity's.

I had lost her twice; I was not going to let the clock run out before on a third opportunity. It was the ultimate Hail Mary, I suppose. But, after all the bad karma that had befallen us in the past sixteen years, all of the stupid decisions and unlucky circumstances that had kept us apart, well, I wasn't going to let a simple matter like the disintegration of the planet's crust or a few gushing rivers of lava scorching the eastern seaboard get in my way.

Of course, I could very well be walking all this way for nothing. After the weather went berserk and the earth's surface started tearing itself apart, well, electronic communications had been the first creature comfort to go (but not the last, if you consider running water, stable infrastructure or easily breathable atmosphere to be creature comforts). So, my chance to reach out to her, to ask her what she was doing with her last moments on earth, had been ruined by a simple matter of technological failure.

Which was a terrible irony, actually, as the Internet had been, during that perfect year, the umbilical that had tied us together, that had pumped our love up and down the east coast and had fueled our dreams of escape, togetherness and happiness. We had first met, of course, in a time before everyone was jacked in and logged on.

Our initial spark had been fanned by more mundane matters: reading printed scripts in a black box theater or visiting the local comic shop once a week. We even watched TV with rabbit ears and rented VHS tapes, believe it or not. Now I would kill for an active electrical outlet, never mind a bootleg copy of a *Red Dwarf* or *The Tomorrow People*.

Of course, I would have to face her as an entirely different person from the one she'd known. After all, during my epic walk, I had killed people. At first it had been in self-defense. As the trappings of society had crumbled along with the surface of the planet, well, let's just say that the mob behavior humans had exhibited in the wake of race riots or football championships paled in comparison to the savagery of Armageddon. I witnessed roving lunatics who wore pieces of human flesh as trophies of their slaughters, and bands of desperate men joined together in the spirit of conquest and a return to the barbaric roots of our ancestors. The first man I shot had been, I think, either trying to rape me or eat me — likely both, though I'm not sure what sequence he'd had in mind. After that, well, it was a lot easier, and the reasons were plentiful: self defense, obtaining what I wanted or needed, removing obstacles from my path or putting people out of their misery. I had as many reasons to kill these days as bullets in my gun.

Besides, I didn't think death had much meaning anymore. I mean, at this point, does it matter if you stick around until the end of the credits? The movie is over already.

But I was hoping beyond hope for one last extra scene, starring me. One final chance to see her again.

I still remembered the first time I saw her, of course. In college, I had a tendency to arrive early to the first session of a new class. I used to tell myself it was because I wanted to be prepared or to talk to the professor or something. I might have even believed it was a symptom of my neuroses (of which there are many, of course) but, really, it was all about checking out the ladies.

I was shy, of course, as most nerds are. I was paralyzed around pretty girls, and I always made excuses not to talk to them (there would be plenty of time, I thought. All the time in the world to get up the courage, that is, unless the world suddenly ended in an atomic holocaust and I was left with a pile of unread books and a broken pair of spectacles). But I enjoyed looking at them and, if I got to class early, I would be able to check out my female class-mates as they arrived. Saying it now sounds a bit creepy, and, to be honest, it probably was.

But as soon as Linda entered the class, I sat bolt upright. the red flush rising in my face.

Not every twenty-one-year-old woman can look good in a pair of sweats and a t-shirt. She did. (And, I would find out later, she was also a knockout in a fancy dress, a pair of jeans or just about any outfit you could imagine. And I imagined quite a few over the years). And the moment I saw her, it was all over for me, and I spent most of the semester arriving to class early enough to get a seat across from her and desperately trying to think up witty comments to make about her writing.

That, of course, was easy. She was a hell of a writer. Much better than me, as a matter of fact.

But she had other passions she wished to pursue back then. She had so many talents — she is, in point of fact, a genius — but her first love was acting. She had brushed fame a few times as a child actor, in commercials, and coming "this close" to roles on the small screen, but she believed she just needed a chance (and I agreed with her) to get out into the world and blaze her own trail.

And, as much as I supported and admired her drive, it was, ultimately, what drove us apart the first time around. It also led, in a roundabout way, to my pet name. She always called me "H " Not "R" for Robert or any other variation of my given name. The H came from a discussion we had, once, walking down 23rd street toward the statue of Albert Einstein, my favorite spot in the District. She had told me of her plans to move to Los Angeles to pursue acting, and I joked that our situation was like that song, "Taxi," the one about two lovers who parted ways, as one pursued a career in acting. "She took off to find the footlights, and I took off to find the sky."

It was, I told her, a song by Mary Chapin. She laughed and corrected me. "Harry," she said. "Right, Mary," I replied. "No, *Harry*. With an 'H.' H, H, H."

She was right, of course (she always was when it came to facts. Good judgment, on the other hand, had eluded us both). So she playfully called me "H" from then on. And, conveniently, it paired nicely with my nickname for her, like a Chianti with some fava beans. I had, in the first few weeks of our class, been under the impression that her name was Belinda. Perhaps I had misheard her name, or maybe I was paying too much attention to her green eyes and wide smile to pay attention. But either way, that's what I called her when she first approached me to be her partner for the dialogue project. She had gently corrected me, "It's just Linda," she said "No 'B.' " I'd tried to play it cool (but, truth be told I'd always been about as cool as the lava flow that had eradicated most of Delaware), trying to pass it off as a stylish affectation, like a clever naming game of my own invention. She didn't buy it, of course, but, as I tried to turn it into a running gag, I started calling her "B" when I was trying to be cute (which was, of course, all the time).

It was, I'll admit, entirely lame. But it had made her smile (she'd confessed once, years later, via an e-mail, that I had seduced her with my awkwardness. Good thing I had that in spades). And so, because I'd never been one to cease an activity that elicited such a pretty smile, I'd called her B in every romantic situation that came about, in both iterations of our romance.

We didn't have many moments of romance, though, that first time around. Our friendship was brief and full of promise the anxiety had hit me hard, and I'd felt like the entire world was at stake.

Now that I was knee deep in the end of the world, though, the quakes and the chaos felt a lot more comforting than the paralyzing fear of romantic rejection.

So, I'd bowed out that night, gone back to stew in my room, without seeing the "special" underwear she'd picked out for the occasion. I'd written a note to B, but she never got to read it, as she decided to leave early for California and skip graduation.

I never thought I'd see her again.

We went on with our lives as the world moved slowly and inexorably toward its demise. Individually, the lives of H and B went into the toilet, as I faced a divorce and the breakup of an engagement, and she faced her own failed engagement and unhappy marriage. Our lives were crumbling even as, unbeknownst to us, the very integrity of the planet was doing likewise.

And then, when things seemed at their worst (back when the definition of "worst" merely meant depression and self-loathing rather than the destruction of civilization), we'd found each other again. Thanks to luck and the Internet, we had connected, as I'd virtually sought her out in a moment of loneliness, asking if she'd remembered a foolish geek who'd called her B.

She did. Or so she claimed.

That started the second act of our doomed love affair. I was hoping we'd have a chance for a third.

But, of course, I was only playing a hunch. I couldn't imagine how the minds of others processed the knowledge that the world was coming to an end, what decisions they made when society crumbled. I'd seen so many iterations of the last day on earth scenario as I walked along the eastern seaboard. I saw suicides of every stripe: hangings, slit-wrists, death by asphyxiation, and bullets to the brain. I'd seen people starve to death from lack of hope and dance themselves to death in drug-fueled orgies of mania. I'd seen gangs formed, and stores looted, cars abandoned and homes stolen.

But I hadn't met anyone else who was taking a six hundred mile journey on foot with only the slightest chance of success. A romantic pipe dream that depended on someone else — someone I hardly knew and hadn't spoken to in years — making the same stupid decision.

But, I figured — what the hell?

I knew that, in my last hours, my last minutes on the planet, what I wanted more than anything was to see her, to find her, to touch her. Our timing had never worked in the past; we'd always missed our connections, we'd never had our moment but maybe, in the last seconds of overtime, we would finally have our chance.

It's what I believed. I just hoped it was what she believed. Since the Internet had ceased to exist, since we hadn't spoken in nearly two years, since, well, since something happened in her life, something inexplicable, something that had caused her to shut off communication with me for good, even when we were on the verge of making a decision, creating a world where we could be together.

And then that world crumbled.

But before that, before she blocked me on social networking sights and refused to talk to me for whatever reason only she understood, we'd talked about "What If?" scenarios. "What if we could take a trip together?" "What if we could live in the same place, in the same city?" "What if the world was overrun by zombies?"

The last seemed the most fanciful, of course. But she was a fan of the genre, from Romero to Kirkman. She'd written stories about the zombie apocalypse that I had suggested she submit to publishers, but she never had. For all her talent, she'd never gotten past the doubt that lingered in her mind, doubt in her own abilities, fear of taking a risk, a chance.

I had the same trait, and that is probably why we were doomed from the start, I suppose.

But in those honest moments, we'd discussed our preferences: our choice for a last meal, our deathbed words that could be captured forever for posterity, and our favorite places on the planet. I'd memorized hers, of course, just as I'd memorized her favorite recipes and lines from her favorite movies. I hoped I knew her well enough to discern what she might do in her final days. I hoped she'd have the same idea as me, that she'd take to the streets, on foot, navigating the terrain of the post-apocalyptic streets, moving inexorably north from her home in Georgia to that one spot in the world that made her happy, to spend her final moments in peace. I hoped she'd make it past the roving gangs, through the strangled streets, and into the city — if it still existed. And I hoped she'd be happy to see me.

In school, when we'd talked on the phone in our beds at night, and later, when we'd chatted on the Internet as we closed out the day, we'd developed a ritual. We wanted, more than anything, to begin and end each day together. So, before hitting the pillow, we'd bid each other a fond adieu. "Good night, H," she'd say to me. "Good night, B," I'd reply. No day seemed complete without that exchange and, once she cut me off, I'd been lost without that nightly anchor. I couldn't imagine ending a single night without it.

And now, more than anything, as we approach the Final Night, I want one more chance to utter those words. If there is even a chance to hear her reply or even to just say them to her one last time, I intend to do so. That's why, when others were in denial, when they imagined the government would step in and stop the looters, that the utility companies would get the power and the phones up and running, and that the egg heads would figure out a way to, I dunno, detonate a nuke in the planet core or reroute an asteroid or something and heal our planet, well, when the rest of the world was running on the fumes of hope, I started walking.

And I am almost there.

The best approach into the city, I'd learned, from the few rational people I'd passed and the binoculars I'd scrounged, was down Connecticut Avenue. Though a vein of rusted out cars and abandoned corpses, it was relatively free of gangs and afforded a navigable path. As I climbed over and around the sad, lonely wreckage of our pathetic excuse for a civilization, I passed reminders of my old life: a comedy club that would have been my first date with Linda, a hotel where I'd wedding-crashed with another girl I'd been trying to impress, one I wasted time on and whose name I barely remembered.

I'd expected to see more devastation in the capital, but from what I'd learned early in my journey, the politicians had fled the city almost immediately, once the sham of government had collapsed. Many had died, I suppose, fleeing to their home states, killed by the death throes of the planet or angry mobs or by their own hands. Washington, DC was, to my surprise, a veritable ghost town. In the end, people had run away from their government, not toward it. When there were no answers to be found in the ivory tower, one tends to flee for the salt mines, I suppose.

It took me far longer than normal to navigate my way to Dupont Circle, passing the coffee shop where she had worked, where I had visited her for "the best scones in the city" (it was the only cover story I could come up with). Now it was little more than a pile of glass, rubble and bone.

I continued along New Hampshire Avenue, past my old apartment, itself nothing more than a crater, as most of Washington Circle had been swallowed up by a minor Cratering Event. I turned, then, to walk down 23rd street, past the State Department, sneering as I went, wondering how everything could have all gone so wrong, so fast, how our leaders could have mishandled the situation, how our scientists had been unable to see it coming.

Or maybe they had seen it coming and hadn't been able to do a thing about it. Sometimes matters are just out of our control. Happiness is beyond our reach.

I passed my old friend, Albert Einstein, whose statue outside the Academy of Science had been toppled and desecrated. People tended to blame the academics more than the decision makers, I suppose. But neither faith nor science nor democracy had been enough to save us.

I then passed the shadow of a former savior as I put the Lincoln Memorial behind me, looping around and heading for the Potomac River. When I had been in the city, Einstein had been my place of refuge. Hers had been nearby, though I hadn't known it at the time. The steps behind the Lincoln Memorial, next to the Memorial Bridge, leading down to the river. She'd called them the symphony steps, as that had been the spot she'd frequented when she watched the symphony float by along the Potomac. It was her spot to sit and think.

And if there was one thing I had learned about her during the two periods of my life when I'd captivated the woman, it's that she loved to think—and over think. I hoped it was what she intended to do with her last moments on earth.

But as I neared my destination, I sensed something. Perhaps it had been my weeks on the road, out in the wilds of the dying earth that had given me a sixth sense, perhaps I was finally losing my mind after weeks of solitude, pushing my body to the limit in pursuit of my fantasy. Perhaps I just knew that time was finally running out.

The earth below me was starting to rumble. I could feel the vibrations through my stolen shoes, rattling my tired and wasted knees. I had seen the remnants of Cratering Events up close, and I'd seen them happen in real-time in the distance. They were happening at an increasing pace, one I had chosen to ignore, as it likely meant that the end was coming, faster and faster, that the chances of achieving my pipe dream were dwindling and my story would likely end like that of millions before me, swallowed up by the planet that had birthed me, eradicating me from its memory like a virus, my fondest desire unfulfilled.

Story of my life.

But even as the earth shook and split around me, I pushed forward. I clambered up and around the rocky protrusions and the groans and protestations of the aching crust threatened to burst my eardrums. Perhaps this was not just my end, a localized event like so many before. Maybe this was the end of us all. If it was, it was welcome. I'd done little with my time on the globe and the same went for the species that had spawned me.

I had failed in so many endeavors already, and, all along, I'd expected to fail at this as well. I never thought I'd make it out of Connecticut, never thought I'd survive the trip through New Jersey. But the entire time, memories of her filled my head, thoughts of smiles and missed opportunities and folly of youth.

Of the encouragement and laughter and passion we'd shared through the Internet, of all those nights in bed, knowing that she was out there, thinking of me as she drifted off to sleep as I was thinking of her. And she'd been all I'd thought about the entire journey. The time we'd had together, the time we'd spoken about sharing in the future, and the time that would be denied to us, as it would be to all others, as the universe went on without the scourge of humanity to spread throughout the cosmos and taint the countless worlds that lay beyond.

Smoke and ash were pouring from the earth as I pushed on toward those steps, as I coughed and choked through the darkening air, the searing heat from the spewing lava blasting my skin and bringing me to the point where I could barely hold on to my consciousness.

I didn't know how long I'd last, but I'd make every second count until… until I was dead and certain she was not coming.

But then, through the haze of the smoke and the fog of my exhausted, protesting mind, I saw something.

A form. A person. A woman.

Sitting on the steps, even as the marble cracked and screamed around her. At peace. Staring out into the water as buildings collapsed along the horizon and the air turned black with soot.

Was it her? Had she really come? Or was it someone else, some other poor, stupid soul with nowhere else to go? Or, perhaps, was the woman's form merely a last, desperate illusion generated by my sad, damaged mind in its final seconds?

I stumbled down the steps toward her, the cries from my mouth swallowed by the screams of the earth. I reached out, put a hand on the small shoulder and turned her face toward me.

And, looking into her eyes, I said the words I'd longed to utter. "Good night, B."

RISING

MARC SHEMMANS

The stars were wonderful tonight. I wanted to reach out and trace Orion with my finger, but my arms were pinned down above my head, and this one was taking twice as long as the others.

As always, I measured the time it took by the number of stars I managed to count. I had already reached one hundred and sixty-six.

It doesn't really matter. The result was always the same.

After two years, I'm not even bothered by the process any-more. When the really violent ones bash my face in, or use rusted knife blades to mark me up, I harden. When I have gun barrels jammed so far down my throat it takes days to get the copper taste off the back of my tongue. I accept it, because I have a purpose, and I have my stars.

I'm Angela Shepherd. I've been raped twenty-four times, not counting this one. I've been cut eleven times, stabbed twice, and beaten more times than I can remember. I was shot in the stomach near Queensway Tunnel a year ago. The only rape that ever hurt, though — *really* hurt — was the first one, the one that gave me AIDS the same year we had the nuclear war.

The war on terror escalated and set off a chain of events no one but a madman could have wanted and which nobody, not even the madmen, could stop. Over a matter of months there were missiles under the earth, in the sky, beneath the waves, and missiles with thermo-nuclear warheads, enough to kill everybody on earth—three times over. Something set them off; sent them flying, west to east and east to west, crossing in the middle like cars on a cable-railway.

East and west, the sirens wailed. Emergency procedures began, hampered here and there by understandable panic. Helpful leaflets were distributed and roads sealed off. VIPs went to their bunkers and volunteers stood at their posts. Suddenly, no one wanted to be a model or a rock-star. Everyone wanted to be one thing: a survivor. But it was an overcrowded profession.

Every town received their individually-programmed warhead. Not one had been left out and they struck, screaming with pin-point accuracy, bursting with blinding flashes, brighter than a thousand suns. Entire towns and city-centers vaporized instantly, while tarmac, trees and houses thirty miles from the explosions burst into flames. Fireballs, expanding in a second to several miles across, melted and devoured all matter that fell within their diameters. Blast-waves, traveling faster than sound, ripped through the suburbs. Houses disintegrated and vanished. So fierce were the flames that they consumed all the oxygen around them, suffocating those people who had sought refuge in deep shelters.

Winds of a hundred and fifty miles an hour, rushing in to fill the vacuum, created fire-storms that howled through the streets, where temperatures in the thousands cooked the subterranean dead. The very earth heaved and shook as the warheads rained down, burst upon one another, and a terrible thunder rent the skies.

For an hour the warheads fell, then ceased. A great silence descended over the land. The Jones were gone, and the Smiths were no more. Through the silence, through the pall of smoke and dust that blackened the sky, trillions of deadly radioactive particles began to fall. They fell soundlessly, settling like an invisible snow on the devastated earth.

Incredibly, here and there, people had survived the bombardment. They lay stunned in the ruins, incapable of thought. Drifting on the wind, the particles sifted in upon them, landing unseen on clothing, skin and hair, so that most of these people would die, too, but slowly.

Most, but not all. There were those whose fate it was to wander the landscape of poisonous desolation. Wander and confront the other survivors.

One of them was me.

He finally finished, smashed a beer bottle against the alley wall, and pressed a sharp piece of glass to my cheek. He said he would take my tongue if I told anyone. I don't know why he said that. *Who on earth would care?* "Anyway, you fucking liked it," he said.

I didn't listen to him, though. My hands were free now, and I traced Orion's bow drawn wide at Taurus. Blood slid over my cheek where the glass dug in and I started to laugh.

"Stupid bitch," he growled. Then he walked into the shadows of the alley. A part of me felt like following and killing him. But I didn't. I knew he would die pretty soon anyway after laying with me.

With AIDS, there are open lesions, and ballooning lymph nodes.

I was lying in broken glass and maggot-covered garbage; it started to rain in pucker marks on the alley floor. I could still smell him—all sour beer and mildewed cigarettes, on my torn clothes. According to our information, I was the fourth girl he'd raped.

I walked up the alley, I held my clothes together in fistfuls, and Brandon came to me out of the darkness like an illusion. His gun was drawn and he carried my first aid bag. "Jesus," he said, "Christ. Nine and a half minutes."

"The rule's ten, Brandon. You know that," I said, and suddenly I was on my elbows and knees, coughing dry, hot air.

I get weak breath.

The rain came down harder and Brandon helped me up and draped his coat over my shoulders. "What'd he cut you with?" he asked me, wiping the blood with a towel from the bag.

"A bottle," I said. "I counted two hundred and twelve."

"I told you, you're his fourth. He's comfortable."

"He's dead. He just doesn't know it." I held the end of an adhesive bandage to my cheek, and Brandon pulled the other end tight and thumbed it down. "Probably wouldn't give a shit, anyway," I said.

"Don't know," Brandon said. "Balls are just balls until you're kicked there. Then, they're your whole goddamn world."

It was after the second time I was raped that I met Brandon. He was the person who found me. Just being around, he seemed to take some of the hurt away, to hoist it onto his shoulders. He rarely spoke except with his eyes, looking out from under his dark hair. What they said was, *I'm sorry this had to happen. I'm sorry this happened to you.*

Someone who was raped, they're raped again every time they're asked about it.

Tell us exactly what happened. Give us the details.

What I remember is the man's rotten teeth. Smiling, saying, "You're my little pussycat, ain't cha?" I remember the large, bruise-colored birthmark around his colorless right eye. "Here kitty, kitty. Here kitty," he said, his spit hitting my face. The sores around his nose and mouth. His breath on my neck.

Details.

I passed out under a monster and woke up with Brandon holding me. They found my attacker six months later in the basement of an abandoned house on Lampkin Lane. What the AIDS left, the rats took.

After the rape, Brandon's eyes said he was hurting. As for me? I couldn't give a shit.

After I was diagnosed positive, I was terrified. Terrified and numb. The doctors tell you all about HIV. They tell you about rapid weight loss and chronic fatigue. Fever and night-sweats. You learn about venereal diseases.

The details.

You're put on a drug treatment called Highly Active Anti-Retroviral Therapy. Called HAART. This is a combination of three HIV drugs: NRTIs, PIs, and NNRTIs. This is what you will feed your body the rest of your life.

Words you can't spell. Words you can't even say.

In the hospital, Brandon never left my side. Even after visiting hours, he was never asked to leave. In that room, in the burning hours of the early mornings, something was growing.

One afternoon, a Social Services agent told me, all smiles, about a family that would take care of me. My first one. This is where I'll go to die until Brandon takes my hand, and said, *I've lost faith in the Justice System. They send a rapist or a pedophile to prison, but what is prison? It's a bed and three hot meals a day. A color TV, weight room and recreational yard. Its state funded programs for better prison libraries and improved inmate education.*

By the time I was twenty, I'd been raped, infected with AIDS and had survived a nuclear war. But Brandon survived the nuclear war, too. And we had a plan.

At the car I changed clothes. I always have extra clothes in the trunk: underwear, shirts, pants, and socks. Even an extra pair of shoes. I put on a hooded jacket, zipped it to my chin, and pulled the hood over my head. I couldn't stop my hands from shaking.

I get chills.

I put my fingers to the heater vent; Brandon put the car into drive. His eyes said, *You look so tired.* Rain pelted his cheek through the open window and slid down his face in black streaks.

"Look," he said, "you did one. Let's call it a night."

I knew this was coming.

I shook my head "We planned two."

"It's so cold." He rubbed his eyes and saw my hands rattling against the heater vents. "You'll get pneumonia again..."

"Brandon..."

"Your body won't hold up this time." He looked out his window. "We could take some time off."

"I told you I'm all right. Just drive."

"Fine." He rubbed his eyes again, shook his head, and laughed. "When people think about living in a world like this it makes them *want* to die."

I laughed.

We turned left on Pilate Street and a black Sedan whipped in behind us. Brandon adjusted the rearview mirror, squinting from the glare of its headlights.

In my mirror, I opened my mouth. I have a thick, yellow tongue now.

Still looking in the rearview, he said. "How did they get that car?"

"The same way we did," I said. "Steal it."

I scrutinized myself in the mirror. With or without AIDS, it's the reflection of someone living in a world that is as doomed as they are."

Our plan consisted of us scouting the city, looking for life. This sometimes took hours, but when we did find them, you could guarantee we'd find gangs: drug dealers, addicts and known felons. It's as though the missiles only killed the decent folks — the honest people and their families. It's as if only the scum survived.

When we found life we kept a distance and took notes.

Imagine a young girl in this new world late at night. Imagine her alone except for her stars and an angry man parked two blocks down, counting the seconds down from ten minutes. Imagine her held face down over a gutted sofa littered with syringes and used needles, her head pulled back by the hair, a knife to her throat.

Imagine a worm on a hook.

And they share their needles and spread themselves around. This is how the disease is injected. Rapists aren't confined to any certain social class. They're not all junkies in wrecked-out heroin houses, or gutter-rats living like zombies in back alleys. Many of them are doctors and bankers, athletes and lawyers.

Number four on my list of twenty-five at one time was a family doctor that sometimes gave sedated female patients a little 'extra' check-up. Number nine was a high school history teacher who gave A's for more than hard study.

Number twenty, a preacher, a husband and father of four, had a thing for young Asian boys. *These* people are easiest to infect. They're the ones who survived and now prowl the streets looking for women or children. However, we go and find their hangouts.

I'm young and attractive. An easy worm on a poisoned hook, and after they finish with me little do they know they'll soon loosen their grip on this world.

Since we began two years ago, six of the twenty-five have died — two from the disease and four suicides. At the bone, this is how our world operates. You have to look after yourself because no one will lookout for you. Do unto others before they do it to you.

Bomb us, we bomb you. Attack. Counterattack.

Then turn the other cheek when you get tired of watching.

I looked back at the headlights of the Sedan. It's been follow-ing us for six miles.

"I'm serious," Brandon said. "We need a few months, just till the weather eases."

"That car's still behind us," I said.

He glanced in the rearview mirror. "I don't think I can keep doing this."

"Then stop. But this was your plan, too."

"We started two years ago. We're even now. And things are different."

"Different? The people we deal with? I say things are worse."

"Maybe we're helping out with that," he said.

"I'm sacrificing myself to get rid of the scum!"

"You're sacrificing yourself for a dead world!"

"There's bound to be some good people left."

"Can you honestly say we've met anyone who fits that descrip-tion since the war?"

I fell silent. I couldn't answer him because I knew he was right.

"You're sacrificing *us*. I know the shit holes you disappear into every night. How you might not walk out." He rubbed his eyes and looked back out the window. "It's killing *me*, too."

We were close to our location. "Pull over," I said.

The Sedan passed us and disappeared into the night. I waited a moment, making sure it didn't return. When I was satisfied it wasn't going to reappear, I looked at Brandon. "Look, what we do, works. We're getting rid of filth every night."

"But we're also wasting what time we have left."

"We have to go sometime," I said, starting to cough. "Mine will be soon." I coughed until I was dry heaving into my jacket sleeve. I wiped my mouth, opened the car door, and Brandon took my arm. I looked at him and I could see there were tears forming in the corners of his eyes.

"Please," he said.

"Just promise," I said, "that when I die, you'll be two blocks away, watching the clock."

He laid his head back. "Be careful."

"See you in ten or less."

He knew it was useless because this was who we were. This was *why* we survived. You couldn't have kept Christ from His cross. And when the nails are in your wrists, you just have to hang.

I walked into the alley.

Three men were hovering around a barrel fire near the end. The alley was lit red like the sunset of a bad love poem. The three men saw me coming toward them through the filmy heat rising off the fire. My jacket hood was slipped over my head and my face was hidden, but my female figure was still easy to make out. They stopped, looked at me. Men were so predictable. Give them the bait and they'll take it every time.

They stepped around the barrel fire and were backlit into silhouettes. Two were short, the other one as tall as Goliath. They surrounded me, then snatched me up and lifted me into the air like an offering — a sacrificial lamb — and carried me to the end of the alley.

Their hands were tearing at my clothes, at the sores on my back and shoulders, and for a second I saw my family, my friends, and my old life and wished to God I was there, not here in this Godforsaken world. They flipped me face-first into a pile of half-opened garbage bags. Rats scattered, hiding somewhere else in the alley.

My jeans were ripped off in a hard jerk, and my knees dropped to the concrete. This was where I closed my eyes and waited and tried to imagine Orion reaching down and lifting me away.

W hen I returned to the car, Brandon was lying on the back seat, drifting in and out of consciousness, wincing in pain. I saw the dark stain on the front of his shirt. Blood. I inspected the wound. He'd been shot.

I slapped his face and eventually he came to. He told me the people in the Sedan had shot him and had siphoned the gas from the car.

"Can you walk?" I asked.

He nodded. I pulled him to his feet and we began walking.

T here was a fading sign in the café window. **Why not try one of our chip-butties?** My guts yearned. We'd been two days on the road and this was Oston. There was no damage here, no bomb damage, I mean. People had been through looting, because all the doors were kicked in and most of the windows were smashed, but no one would waste a bomb on Oston.

I looked at Brandon. "Why don't we try one of their chip-butties?" I said.

"Shut up." His feet hurt and it was cold as hell.

"Can't we stay here, Brandon? I'm tired. We've been walking all day."

It was about three in the afternoon. We'd spent the previous day walking after I managed to remove the bullet from Brandon's chest. Then I dressed it as well I could with our make-shift First Aid kit.

Last night we'd discovered a farm building and had found a pile of rock-hard *swedes* in a corner. We'd gnawed on some of the turnip-looking vegetables for breakfast. They were like doorknobs, but it was the first decent meal we'd had in weeks.

"I reckon we can spend the night. Doesn't look like anyone's around."

We'd come halfway down the main street by now, peering in doorways and down alleyways. Nothing stirred, not even a cat.

I nodded towards a house with its windows still intact. "We'll hole up in there. Hang on a minute." I left him standing in the middle of the road and approached the house. No smell of occupation reached my nostrils, only the damp, flat odor of decay. I entered and did a quick tour of the rooms. There was a beat-up suite, a rusting gas-cooker and some junk on the floors, broken cups and dishes. Two upstairs rooms had beds, but looters had taken the mattresses and bedding.

It had been a pretty rudimentary café, a hikers' place with a juke-box and cheap plastic furniture. The juke-box stood rusting in a corner and someone had smashed all the furniture. The display counter was glassless, the tea and coffee machines ripped out. I hadn't expected to find anything here; it was the cellar that interested me. I found the steps, pulled a flashlight from my pocket, and went down.

It was a single cellar, whitewashed, with tiers of shelving around the walls. I flashed the light about. The shelves were bare, except that on the top one, in a corner, stood the gas-meter I'd been looking for. I went over, reached up and thrust my hand behind it. As I'd hoped, there was something in the cobwebbed space between the meter and the wall. If stock is piled on a shelf near a meter, something is bound to fall down behind it now and then. It was always happening at my home.

On tiptoe, I pulled out two rusty tins and a damp, disintegrating packet.

The packet had contained breakfast cereal, but now held only a lump of mold. I dropped it on the floor and examined the tins. The labels were damp and spotted with black, but enough of the print remained for me to see that one was soup and the other spaghetti. I grinned, and thrust the tins in my pockets, grabbed my flashlight, and was halfway up the steps when a pair of legs in black denim appeared at the top.

"Stop right there!"

I stopped, feeling myself go cold. The legs weren't familiar, but the voice was. It was a tall man with graying hair and a toothless grin. He held a submachine gun.

A second man appeared with a flashlight, which he shone in my face. I jerked my head aside, squinting from the glare, and the tall man said, "Well, well, well, if it isn't a nice young girl for us. What're you doing roaming about the countryside, eh?"

I was scared, and hadn't expected to be going about business today.

He waved me up to the main floor and off the stairs. "Right. Over against the wall. Turn your pockets out."

He'd seen the bulges. I pulled out the tins and my flashlight, and his mate came and took them from me. I leaned my back against the wall. A few flakes of paint fluttered down and settled on my jacket. My hair brushed the underside of a shelf. I felt tired.

"Goodbye, Brandon," I whispered and closed my eyes.

The submachine gun made a terrific racket in the confined space. They say you don't hear the one that gets you, but I wouldn't know about that. All I know is, there was this hellish clatter and I stiffened, but nothing hit me. I opened my eyes and Brandon was on the steps with a gun, and the two men were lying on the floor, dead.

"What happened?" I asked.

"I heard them coming towards the café; three of them. They'd seen us, I suppose. I saw two of them go in. They left the other one watching the bikes they rode in on. They hadn't seen me so I got my club, sneaked up, and belted him over the head. I took his gun."

I smiled. "Let's get something to eat."

"More will come. We need to get out of here now! Follow me."

There's a sort of instinct for self-preservation that goes on operating long after you've stopped caring. As I followed Brandon, a part of me wished he hadn't saved me from those men, that he'd left me to die.

We left the village and walked uphill, avoiding the road. We walked hand in hand. My strength was leaking away, but this was one last journey I had to make. Neither of us spoke; being alone said enough.

Around dawn, we saw a house. It was hidden from Oston by a fold in the hills.

After a while, we walked slowly, steadily up the incline to the house where we hugged and kissed.

"What're you doing?" I asked him.

"I don't want to put up with this anymore," he said. "I want to leave it all behind."

He stroked my face and my neck, then kissed me once more. We made love all night, knowing that this was it, that we had reached the end of the road.

Afterwards, we sat in the back garden and watched the sky to the east, which was a deep blue now, and a sliver of sun became visible on the horizon, blindingly bright.

I suddenly didn't feel too well. "Brandon," I whispered. I felt sick and already my senses were beginning to withdraw. I knew what it meant.

"I'm here. I'm here with you," he said and picked up the gun.

"Listen...listen to me..."

"I'm listening."

"I don't want to breathe another second..."

"I don't think I can continue without you," he said. "The world will be such a dark, horrible place without you."

"Hold me tight," I said, tears running down my cheeks.

I felt my death approach. I winced, gasped in pain, but never cried out.

By the time the sun broke from the horizon, I was gone.

EARTH'S END

ANTHONY GIANGREGORIO

Journal entry 366

It was the one year anniversary of World War 3 yesterday. Too bad I didn't have a cake, would have celebrated, as morbid a thing as that sounds.

I've been trapped in this bomb shelter for exactly one year and one day, and it looks like I'll have to leave, whether I like it or not.

I've run out of food and water, though I've been rationing it for more than six months. I'm skin and bones and I sleep most of the time. I miss my family. I miss Tina and the kids.

They were visiting Tina's mother when the bombs first began to fall. It happened so fast, there was no way for them to get home. I wonder if they're alive out there. I have to believe they are. With no windows, I have no idea what's going on outside and above my small prison. For all I know, everything is fine, but I highly doubt it. Besides, if it was fine, Tina would have knocked on the hatch and told me to get out and stop being silly.

You know, it's funny. When I bought my house and found out there was a 1950's bomb shelter at the back of the land, I'd laughed about it. The plan had been to dig it up, but when I found out the cost, I decided to leave it where it was. Besides, it was piece of history. It was something fun to show guests when they came to the house for the first time.

Who would ever have imagined I would actually need the damn thing to live in? Not me, that was for sure. I'm just glad I never bothered to remove the dried food stores and water that was stockpiled in the back of the shelter. If I did, well, let's just say I wouldn't be writing this.

I literally jumped inside the hatch and slammed it shut while the bombs hit Boston repeatedly. The entire shelter had shaken as the earth shook from the impacts. Dust had rained down on my head and I wondered if one of those missiles would hit close to me and end it all right then. Looking back, that might have been for the best.

There had been a small, AM/FM radio in the shelter with a hand-crank on its side to charge the batteries, and at first I managed to get some chatter on it. The reports weren't good. The East Coast had been bombarded with missiles armed with nuclear warheads, and the West Coast had fared little better. The Midwest had done slightly better, as whoever had sent their missiles knew that was where we grew most of our food. But still, it was pretty bad there as well. All major cities were struck at least once, and cities like New York, Philadelphia, Boston and Chicago, were pounded into oblivion, as if it was to make a statement.

Though wracked with guilt and worry over my family, at least with the radio, I felt somewhat connected with the rest of the world, but then, three months in, I woke up, turned it on and there was nothing but static on all channels.

Then it became intolerable and more than once I almost opened the hatch and left, but people on the radio had said the radiation level was high and that if you had a choice, stay indoors.

So with every fiber of my being wanting to leave the shelter and search for my wife and kids, I didn't, I stayed put...and waited.

Each night as I slept, images of what had happened to Tina and the kids came to me. I imagined her hearing the massive explosions when the missiles hit and going out onto her mother's front porch, our two boys right behind her. Seven and eight years of age, they would be as curious as her and willful to the point that if she told them to stay inside they would have ignored her.

they would have stood on that porch, looking out where the city was miles away, seeing the mushroom clouds as they sprouted into the sky, and then suddenly there would be a flash of light and the blast would roll across the city and into the suburbs, burning everything in its path to cinder. I think about how they would be frozen in time for one brief instant as the firestorm rolled over them and then *poof*, they were gone, vaporized into nonexistence.

I would wake up crying then, screaming to the darkness that it wasn't fair.

It never goes away you know, the loss, the grief. They say it does, but it doesn't. That hole in your soul is always there, always empty. Maybe it's not as big as it was upon first learning your loved ones are dead but it's there, always there.

After the radio went out it became more difficult to deal with my situation. Alone with only my thoughts, I couldn't help but think of the worst case scenarios. Was anyone even alive out there now? Or had radiation finally killed them all.

I almost went mad and I very well might have if not for me finding this journal, which was blank when I first discovered it. The first few pages were filled with the inventory of the shelter and the original owner had used it for that, but to me, it became a lifeline, a way for me to put my thoughts on paper, so that they didn't pile up in my head until my skull exploded.

I went back to day one when I arrived and wrote down what I remembered of those days and I have to be honest, many of the days near the beginning were mostly a blur. But I tried. Then, once I had caught up, I began writing in more detail, such as this entry today.

But you see, whoever might read this one day if you find my shelter, this entry is so very important because it will be my last. I've decided to take what meager supplies I have left and head out tomorrow, before I'm so weak from hunger I won't have any strength to climb the ladder to the surface hatch, let alone travel.

What I'll find out there is a mystery but I know I'll die if I stay in this shelter so I really have no choice. It's easy to take a chance when there are no other options before you.

My first goal will be to find other people, and hopefully they can help me find my wife and kids. If my family is alive out there, and they somehow have survived for a year after the bombs, I swear to God, I'll find them.

Brett Mitchell

The hatch opened on the bomb shelter and Brett emerged, blinking his eyes repeatedly at the harsh sun. The sky was deep red — the color of blood — the clouds hanging low, looking like massive pillows of burnt orange. Before him was nothing but debris, a wasteland of ruined homes, houses, vehicles and stores.

He slowly began to swivel his head, taking in his surroundings. It was as he turned his head so that he was looking behind him that his eyes went wide and he said, "Oh, hello, who are you?"

The man standing before him didn't reply. The man had been startled when the hatch had opened, as if not sure what was happening, but in less than a second he'd come to the conclusion that someone was emerging from some sort of hidden bunker.

"My name's Brett," Brett said to the man as the dark figure pushed back the long black coat he was wearing, pulled out a massive Smith and Wesson revolver, and without so much as a twitch of hesitation, shot Brett in the chest.

His mouth wide-open in consternation, Brett went flying backwards to land on a mound of rubble. As blood seeped into the earth beneath him and he spit bloody red bubbles, his vision fading fast, Brett saw the man pull out a long butcher's knife and step towards him, a hungry smile on the man's face.

SUFFER THE END

VINCENZO BILOF

Father John Roland was well aware that the apocalypse was his fault.

Between the guilt that manifested itself through the tremulous, almost ritualistic, shaking of his hands, the constant prodding of his nemesis Beelzebub, and his own Catholic inclination to self-loathe, Father Roland understood he was responsible for civilization's tragic and abrupt conclusion.

This certain knowledge regarding his horrific mistakes did not deter him from maintaining his relationship with Christ, and it was this relationship that made him feel he had an opportunity to save the human race and usher in an era of renewed, majestic faith.

Walking beneath a sundered, crimson sky that seemed to mirror the rivers and oceans of blood that had replaced the world's prominent water sources, Father Roland stalked amongst the ruins, clutching his mother's rosary in his fist. He'd avoided most major cities, but in order to confront Beelzebub at last, he would have to witness the horrors of the world's end for the first time. His lips moved in rhythmic prayer, and his fist shook uncontrollably.

Beelzebub's persistent nagging hounded him throughout the ruins, reminding him of his abysmal failure.

"Mary doesn't hear you, John. She's being violated by a brigade of angels. But this is what goes on behind the Pearly Gates. They never told you, did they?"

Beelzebub was his constant companion, the familiar that haunted his travels toward that distant, eldritch tower erected to honor the foul demon's ascension over mankind.

The screaming steel foundations of burn-out, windowless structures echoed throughout that otherwise silent dreamscape; their collapse into clouds of dust and ash seemed a constant storm of destruction.

Father Roland's well-worn boots crunched on shards of broken glass while a conglomeration of dust and ash stung his eyes, blown by a light wind. Winged serpentine creatures with prehensile tails and long, slavering jaws beat their bat-like wings above the wasteland, searching for mortal prey.

Demoniac skeletons shepherded long lines of enslaved souls wearing silver collars around their necks, their eyes downcast while the eight-foot-tall caricatures of bone and nightmare marched them through piles of crumbled masonry.

Father Roland walked among them untouched, invisible from the glaring red eyes of those terrible monstrosities.

"Don't worry, Johnny boy, you're still cursed. You're my beloved pet and this is your eternity; forever doomed to live in the world that you helped destroy. Look at those sad mortals, my friend. Aren't they simply pitiful?"

Cackling, powerful laughter stopped Father Roland in his tracks. He closed his eyes and gripped the rosary tightly in his grasp. Against the reverberating mockery resounding in his consciousness, Father Roland conjured images of his mother, sitting in her patio chair, looking out across the sparkling blue water of Lake Michigan with a smile painted on her face.

Father Roland couldn't help but stand in awe of the awful, massive construct that had risen out of the ruins. Beelzebub's cylindrical tower rose thousands of feet into the air into the blood-red, mist-heavy atmosphere. The rows of skulls forming the outer walls seemed to glow as if they were slow-dying embers.

The foul smell of an ancient putrescence amid the waves of heat pounding the air around the tower served as the only unnatural barriers that could prevent Father Roland from walking in unchallenged.

He understood the real reason why Beelzebub's power couldn't touch him: his absolute faith in God provided him with a spiritual barrier against the damnable taint of evil that had enslaved the world.

It was this faith that would allow him to overthrow Beelzebub once and for all, and restore mankind's faith in God. After all, he'd helped destroy the world in the first place. Now it was time for Him to reap what he sowed.

There were very few hours that passed in the torturously-long days in which Father Roland was not reminded of his horrific mistakes. The very moment that had brought a cataclysmic end to world economies and global armies remained fresh in his mind, although the memory was aided by Beelzebub's insistence.

Father Roland had always been a vigorous missionary, whose faith in the grace of Christ and His glorious message had brought him face-to-face on numerous occasions with the impoverished and the suffering. Fresh out of seminary school, he'd worked in the ghettoes of Detroit to help cleanse the soul-rending addictions that had taken hold of youths who could still have a promising future ahead of them.

When an opportunity to visit Africa presented itself, Father Roland excitedly made the long journey into the tropical, forested jungles, where children suffered from malnutrition, war, and disease.

Nothing could have prepared him for the frightened visages of the dying and the suffering. Long, sweaty nights spent delivering the final sacrament to skeletal parentless children was the most common application of his faith and services. In his spare time, he often knelt and reaffirmed his faith and purpose by promising God he would always do his best and never question His way.

The body count continued to rise, despite all of his efforts. He began to consider himself more of a soul-shepherd, a man whose only true duty was to pray for the dying in words they couldn't comprehend, words that ultimately meant nothing to them.

The deepest depths of his haunted consciousness assaulted him in the evenings with nightmare imagery.

He would find himself standing before an altar, his arms outstretched, the perpetual sweat staining his brow and collar present during his sermon. He stood under the gaze of a powerfully ruined church, with the sacred imagery depicted in stained glass windows, forever cracked and shattered. His voice echoed amongst a congregation sitting patiently in broken, leaning pews covered in the dust of centuries. The statuesque corpses of the semi-nude congregation did not have eyes set in their skulls, and their lips were an icy blue.

He'd been asleep, at the mercy of those unreal corpses that reminded him of his inability to alleviate the personal suffering endured by the innocent and diseased children, when a knock at his door roused him from slumber.

A French nun stood outside of the door as a torrential downpour misted over the darkness beyond her. She spoke in fragmented English. The words he could understand would forever change the fate of mankind. She'd told him that one of the younger boys awoke suddenly in the night, blubbering words in English that the nun could barely understand.

Father Roland was the only priest present at the encampment; the others had gone into town and would return early the next morning.

He hurriedly dressed himself and followed her through the tempest, trudging through mud in an abyssal, cavernous darkness. For a moment, he thought he lost the French nun, but he kept his eyes forward and followed her into the makeshift hospital, where a strange alliance of doctors from a myriad of countries stood in the lobby, waiting for him.

Their brows were furrowed with heavy alarm and frustration, the mark of professionals whose expensive education and experience proved useless. They led Father Roland through the hospital's narrow corridor, past rooms where the smell of feces, vomit and decay was capable of overwhelming the most experienced priest's fortitude.

The boy's name was Kibwe; he was a parentless malaria sufferer, brought to the encampment by a local tribe. The locals often deposited their sick amongst the white people, as if the children were cursed by a horrific and ancient magic.

Large flies annoyingly buzzed all around the corners of the room, accompanied by the familiar smell of looming death. Father Roland stood with the procession of foreign doctors, which included the French nun who'd retrieved him.

Kibwe immediately sat up and spoke in a husky and aged adult voice, "*Ah, the useless Father Roland. How've you been sleeping lately, John? Have you been masturbating to the screams of the dying girls that you can't save? You're failing them on purpose, aren't you, Johnny boy?*"

Father Roland clenched his fists and courageously stood firm, as flies perched upon the back of his sweaty neck. Rain continued to pound noisily outside.

He didn't curse his misfortune, nor did he second guess what he himself had just witnessed. He performed the sign of the cross and produced his mother's rosary from his pocket.

Kibwe spat with precise aim upon the rosary. "*To Hell with you and your faith!*" Kibwe's skeletal, malnourished body quaked with laughter. "*Do you know what your mother has been up to? She screams your name! She screams for the son who abandoned her. She's told us so much about you."*

Father Roland ignored the thing that was not Kibwe, instead reciting the Lord's Prayer. Kibwe jolted backward and grimaced in pain, writhing on that soiled bed while Father continued to pray.

He stopped and gave the French nun explicit directions to retrieve the things he would need. The doctors stared at him wide-eyed, but before he could explain his intentions, the possessed boy sat up from the bed with his mouth open.

A river of maggots coalesced out of his wide-open mouth.

As Father Roland wrapped the purple stole around his neck and clutched the book in his fist, he ignored the nun's pleas. There was no time to wait for the more experienced priests to return from town. While the doctors tried to subdue Kibwe with tranquilizers and leather straps, Father Roland knew better.

He had an opportunity to save one young man from the clutches of evil amidst all of his other personal failures, and he would stop at nothing to ensure the boy was safe.

Father Roland returned to Kibwe's room alone. As inexperienced as he was in such matters, the priest believed his faith in Christ was enough to give him the strength to triumph over absolute evil.

Sadly, he couldn't have been more wrong.

"You're so eager to help!" the creature taunted him while it wrestled with the straps keeping it prostrate. *"Don't you know that you're a joke? Don't you know that your good friend Jesus laughs at all of your failures? He can't wait to see you screw this one up! Go on, Father, try and save the boy!"*

Father Roland waved flies from his face and began the exorcism rite. His determination and resolve kept him focused on his task, for there was no time to be awed by the torments the creature inflicted on the boy's body. The rain provided good background music for the writhing creature's protests and admonishments.

The strength of his faith filled him, keeping him upright against the savage wailing and obscenities. His concentration and focus were intense — exorcisms required absolute faith and will — and he opened his heart and mind to Christ's magnificent power.

He blinked and found himself standing behind the altar in the nightmare-realm residing within his subconscious. The book and his vial of holy water were before him.

Father Roland looked up, blinked, and found himself standing before that familiar assemblage of desiccated, hopeless corpses, the eyeless youths whose lives he'd failed when they needed him most.

Blinking furiously, he stopped and stood before the dead and watched as they rose in unison.

They were skeletal, fleshless monstrosities from the waist down. The demon's voice echoed through the ruined church.

"When was the last time you went to confession, Father Roland?" the boy's altered voice asked. *"Why are you so surprised? Isn't this what you've seen in all of the movies? Isn't this supposed to happen during an exorcism? I know you've prepared yourself for all of this, haven't you?"*

Father Roland knew he shouldn't acknowledge the creature. Instead, he proceeded with the rite, stretching out his arms, the perspiration on his forehead and under his arms cold and unwelcome.

He understood that the demon was attempting to use its horrendous power on him, and he refused to succumb.

"I've been to a few of these get-togethers before, you know," the creature continued.

The dead gathered in the aisle, bumping into one another. There was one that didn't belong.

One of the dead spirits passed under a foul, gray light filtering through the damaged stained-glass windows.

A mane of wiry, tangled gray hair framed a shriveled visage complete with shining white eyes that did not blink, and black, rotted teeth set within a lipless jaw.

A feminine, familiar voice spoke in the glow of that eerie light. *"Do you remember your dead mother, Johnny?"*

Yes, he did.

Fatherless years spent in low-cost housing with a mother who had to sell her body on the street just to serve her son cold meals.

The only way out of his suffering was through the discovery of Christ, and as he grew older, he learned how to resent the woman whose only ambition in life was to feed her son so he might survive their torrid living conditions and become something greater.

As a teenager, his ability to detest her lusty lifestyle further cemented his commitment to faith.

She came to Sunday Mass when he labored as a common altar boy, though he loathed her profane presence in that holy sanctuary.

It was all he could do to hide his shame; he never permitted others to meet his mother.

She became sick near the end of his secondary education. After he had acquired enough government aid to leave for seminary school, he thought he was leaving her behind for good. He visited on the holidays, but every time he saw her, she seemed weaker, more frail; needy.

Their conversations were difficult and he found it impossible to include her in his prayers. As much as he endorsed some kind of medical assistance for her, she resisted.

When he received the call that she'd died from her untreated syphilis, he was nearing the end of the semester; exams threatened. He shuddered to think about the time he would waste at her funeral. She was a victim of her own vices at last.

His inheritance came to him in the mail—a single, slender package. Inside was a rosary she'd made by hand. He'd held on to it for a long time before finally surrendering to bouts of weeping.

Even then, in his moment of weakness, he lacked all strength to pray for forgiveness.

The benign corpse that shambled toward him in his mother's likeness announced, "*Victoria was such a slut, Father Roland. She gave blowjobs so she could buy you a Happy Meal. I'm sure you know where she is now. But you can save her, Johnny. I'm going to give you the second chance you've always wanted!*"

Father Roland's eyes drifted back to the world in front of him. The dead clustered around the front of the altar, their blue lips opening over black teeth.

"*All you have to do, Father, is take my hand and tell me that I can have the boy. It's a fair trade, is it not? Give me the diseased boy, and the whore doesn't have to burn anymore.*"

Father Roland wanted to protest, to say only God had that power, but as those eager hands reached for him, the fingertips brushing against his face, he reared back and stepped away from the book.

"*Don't fail her again, Father.*" The demon was lying to him.

The Lord's Prayer stumbled weakly through Father Roland's lips, and he held tightly to his mother's rosary.

All of the fear he should have felt before now decimated his sense of duty to God, and he tried to step back from the altar and the mob seeking him.

He kept telling himself they couldn't hurt him, that the spectral manifestations of his own fear were a corruption of his consciousness at the hands of an evil monstrosity, nothing more.

The corporeal realm desired an awful vengeance; it was his lot to suffer at the hands of his guilt and the awful prowess of the benign beasts that ruled over the damned.

Victoria reached for his face and began tearing away strips of bloody flesh.

Father Roland fell backward, and the rosary slid from his fingers. The dead converged upon him, their unholy putrescence filling his nostrils and sickening his stomach. Their fingers clutched at his limbs and pulled at him.

"See how they adore you."

He called out for his mother.

Victoria clapped her bloody hands together as flaps of skin hung loosely over her gory face.

"Tell her that you love her! Tell her that you'll save her soul! Make the trade."

Father Roland threw up his hands. "I don't have that power!"

"You and I have a personal connection, Father Roland. You're an impure priest with skeletons in the closet. All you have to do is tell me that Kibwe belongs to me. Say it, and you can redeem yourself, Father!"

He knew he was defeated, and the unwanted, warm tears filling his eyes were the result of his betrayal and selfish sacrifice.

He lacked the same strength that Christ had when he gave his own life to save mankind.

He said the words.

It was then that Father Roland watched the world end.

Father Roland felt as if his scream was heard around the globe.

"You may call me Beelzebub," the demon said through Victoria's grim countenance.

The corpses withdrew their hands, and the church's roof separated and opened itself to reveal a scarlet sky that rippled with horrific images.

"This is what you've released, Johnny."

Arcane, gigantic creatures stalked amongst the skyscrapers in the sprawling metropolises, swinging massive fists and stomping on unlucky passersby while jet planes vainly fired volley after volley of missiles into those giant beasts.

The images shifted.

Shambling corpses stalked and ravaged an outdoor music festival.

Chaotic screams of anguish and torment rained down from the ethereal sky.

Father Roland couldn't help but watch.

An aircraft carrier in the middle of the ocean, wrapped within massive, constricting tentacles, that squeezed and crunched steel and armaments.

Sailors leapt overboard, while the aircraft carrier was pulled to the depths of the sea.

He had to tell himself that it wasn't real, that this was another of the demon's tricks.

"You can't look away. This is your masterpiece. All I ever needed was complete possession of one human soul, and the meddling of a damaged priest. Your actions are defined by guilt and shame, not by faith. You've been running from your lovely mother your entire life. You're pathetic."

The fallen priest buried his head into his hands in an effort to escape the personal hell in which he now found himself in. Beelzebub's cackling laughter overpowered the whimpering priest's begging and pleading.

Father Roland had to believe he'd simply succumbed to the demon's power — it simply wasn't possible that the exorcism rite could have backfired so badly as to allow Hell sovereignty on Earth.

When he removed his hands from his face, Father Roland found himself lying on the cold floor of the very room in which he'd attempted to pry the demon's strength away from the soul of the innocent Kibwe.

A suffocating darkness strangled all color from the world, and while he pushed himself to his feet, he brushed dust from his aged robes.

A pile of bones rested on the bed where Kibwe had been.

The rest of the hospital was vacant, and his ragged breathing was the only sound in the ghostly necropolis.

As he cautiously made his way down the lengthy corridor, he spied more decaying, dried corpses forever resting upon the beds where they'd suffered the final indignities of the flesh.

Flies flitted casually between rooms, their rampant buzzing accompanying the hysterical fit of sobbing that overtook
Father Roland when he took his first steps out of the hospital, his maddening protests echoing throughout the empty world.

He collapsed to his knees and clasped his hands together tightly.

He closed his eyes and shook his head, then reopened them to find his vision of the new world unchanged.

A deep red sky had replaced the serene blue that should have been above him, while all around him, the village lay smoldering.

A monolithic, perception-consuming tower soared into that red miasma above the physical world, reaching towards invisible heights.

"It happened, Johnny. Your mother is so very proud of you."

Father Roland knew it was his faith that had kept him alive. Roving bands of survivors traversed the scoured wasteland that had once been Africa. They claimed they could not be touched or tainted by the violent monstrosities populating the landscape. The same people belonged to a variety of faiths, but they had one belief holding them together, despite the wreckage that was once their civilization.

The survivors believed in a word — and that word was God.

The appearance of Hell didn't shake Father Roland's belief. In fact, the fall of mankind validated his need for God. A faithless man might have ended his own life in such circumstances, and while the guilt certainly weighed heavily on his shoulders, it wasn't up to him to decide when his life should end.

He also understood His plan might include such a horrific twist on the evolution of mankind. After all, once Beelzebub was finally vanquished, a world of resolute faithful would remain behind to inherit the world.

Father Roland accepted that this was his true mission: to destroy the terrifying evil and restore God's kingdom in the realm that rightfully belonged to Him.

The stalwart priest stepped into the hellish tower, where the echoing screams of mortal men were not enough to deter him. He was able to recognize that fear had been the demon's most powerful weapon, and he would now have to suffer the conceit of human agony that his blind resolve had brought to Earth.

"You've always wanted to serve God, yet you betrayed Him. How does that feel?"

Father Roland smiled thinly. More than anything, Beelzebub's chiding had become an interesting game in which the demon would predictably attack his sense of guilt and self-worth.

The tower was nothing more than one long, winding staircase, one that stood as a testament to the benign tormentor's egotistical nature.

Other foul beasts claiming allegiance to one of man's classical adversaries were absent during the priest's climb, though he was witness to the sinister machinations designed to test both Father Roland's fortitude and the endurance of the human soul.

An assembly of small children sat on their knees upon the steps, their fingers planted firmly in their eyes sockets, fresh blood running thickly down their concave cheekbones. They cried out for Father Roland to save them.

He pressed on.

"Say a prayer for them at least, you selfish prick."

All manner of horrific imagery threatened his fragile courage. He stepped in pools of blood and turned his face away from the various temptations. Each suffering individual needed his prayers and reassurances, but he understood that his own mind might have been afflicted by the demon's power and he must not succumb.

He pressed on.

The red sky seemed to stretch forever, and the steps assaulted his vigor, but he continued, because he knew faltering was not an option.

"Who is it that you want to redeem? Yourself, or these people? Do you think that this tower has an end? Do you think that I would assume some physical form and rule here? I know what you think you can accomplish, and it's amusing...so damn amusing."

He couldn't stop. Not now, not when he was so close. There was no reason for him to suspect his faith in Christ's power would fail him now, in his moment of triumph.

Nude and nubile, a slender woman descended the staircase before him. He kept his eyes on her for too long, because the tired breasts and thin gray hair belonged to the mortal form that had been his mother in her final days.

The rosary in his fist shook, and he stopped in his tracks.

"You said she'd be *released!*" Father Roland shouted, even though he was more the fool for believing a demon's lies.

The ghastly, nude caricature approached and reached for his face. He stood, helpless against the power of his guilt as fresh, warm tears raced down his cheeks.

"I belong here, Johnny," Victoria said.

The Lord's Prayer struggled its way out of his tremulous mouth.

"You've been running for so long. Isn't this what you've always wanted? I know I'm the only woman you can ever love. Why else would you remain chaste? You loved me so much you couldn't bear to be with me. You needed me, but you were ashamed to say it. If you'd told me, I would have given myself to you. I would have done anything to make you happy." She wrapped her thin arms around his shoulders and pressed herself against him. "You never even said goodbye," she said. "I've missed you. I did everything for you, but you're the only man I've ever loved."

His entire body seemed to shake. Every fiber in his body wanted to surrender; he'd never had the strength to combat Hell, as he'd never had the strength to face his own shame.

"Tell me that you love me," his mother said.

He opened his mouth to scream.

The rosary finally slipped from his fingers, and his wavering vision went dark.

Father Roland awoke with his arms stretched across the tattered arms of a reclining chair in his mother's living room. He wiped sleep out of his eyes and loosened his collar.

The idea that he'd abandoned his mother in her final hours was too much to bear.

He'd found the power to forgive her, and once he arrived in her home, he prayed for her daily. It had been a week since she summoned him, and it was all he could do to watch her in the final throes of horror and madness.

Standing on the threshold of her bedroom, he looked in on her long-suffering and emaciated body. She was close to death, and she'd refused any medical treatment.

It was her wish to die here, with her son beside her. She told him that his forgiveness was the only thing she'd wanted during her long and sufferable life.

The blinds on the window were drawn against the sunlight, shading the room in variations of amber. The smell of dust and body waste intermingled with the stifling, airless atmosphere that was reminiscent of those humid, hopeless rooms in the middle of Africa.

Africa...yes, he'd been there, after all. His mind was hazy, and the sequence of events that had brought him back to his mother at last was lost to him, though he attributed to this the fact that he'd just awakened from a disturbing afternoon nap.

The time was drawing nigh. He knew he'd made the right decision. Coming to terms with his mother's failures was enough to reconcile his destiny as one of God's messengers.

His guilt had allowed the impossible dream to overcome him and unleash some metaphorical equivalent to Hell upon his consciousness. It was what he'd always feared, and God had given him the dream to show him that he had made the right decisions.

He knelt beside the bed to deliver the final sacrament unto her, and withdrew a rosary from his pocket. He held it in between his fingers, and realized that it was the same one he'd held in his nightmare. Victoria had made it for him, and it had been delivered to him after her death.

Cool perspiration appeared on his forehead and his hands began to shake, as he struggled to stand, his heart racing. It was only a dream—no man had the power to bring Hell to Earth, and no man had the ability to exchange souls with demonic powers.

After he opened the blinds to reveal a blood-red sky, his mother's altered voice spoke from the bed, as a dark cloud of flies assaulted the ceiling.

"You thought your faith could save you from terror and from suffering. Do you have anything to say for yourself? A prayer, perhaps?"

The failed priest opened his mouth and gasped.

His mother laughed *"I suppose Hell is what you make of it, after all,"* she said with a wide grin.

Father Roland's savage scream was louder than Beelzebub's cackling laughter.

DEAD FRONTIER

TONY GARCIA

Every decision, no matter its origin or intended purpose, inevitably, irrevocably, and unashamedly engulfs the future...and people are stupid.

Clay...brown, cracked and dead stretched in all directions around me, surrounding me, reminding me. In the distance there is a range of low hills equally dead and just before those hills there lies a mockery of civilization. They call it, ironically, Sweet Valley, a cesspool built of scavenged parts, each building leaning against the other, threatening to crumble down any minute. Worse than the buildings are the vermin, remnants of mankind that inhabits them.

Between all of that beauty and me is what really has my attention. Smoke, fire, and screams permeate the red-gray sky while a warm, unpleasant breeze carries the scent of death.

Marauders. What a stupid term, but like everything else, originality died a long time ago. They should just call themselves scum, it would be more accurate. They scavenge and destroy anything worth a damn just to tear it down. This is the future of mankind, undignified self-destruction.

Four of them were taking turns ravaging a woman atop the remains of what looked to be a man and possibly a child. There was a time when slaughtering vermin like these brought me pleasure, now it was just a reflex.

In the span of a thought I'm upon them, fingers outstretched like claws, tearing throats as easy as paper and nearly decapitating with each strike to give a much deserved death to the parasites feeding off the core of the earth. A kick shatters ribs straight through the heart and a flick of my wrist snaps the last bastard's neck. To these men I am death, to the woman now covered in their gore I'm a bizarre, macabre miracle. To me this was a dull choreographed dance I've performed countless times.

Showered in the blood of her assailants, she stares up at me in bewilderment mixed with no small measure of fear. I wonder what she sees. Am I a savior, dark saint, monster, avenging angel, or maybe all of them combined? Shreds of black and brown clothing cling to my lean form loosely, covered by a tattered coat. Large goggles conceal my eyes and a dirty brown scarf covers my mouth. A ragged black hat with a wide brim shadows my face while blood drips from my fingers, mingling with the ever-thirsty earth at her feet. Given all that, I can probably count out the angel imagery.

I remove my goggles and she stares deep into their black depths. Like a deer staring at headlights, she knows she should run, every fiber of her brain screams it, but her body refuses to react. She doesn't even twitch when I pull the scarf away, revealing alabaster skin lined with black veins. A tear rolls down her cheek as my extended canine teeth come into view and she knows death will claim her today after all.

Why did I save her just to kill her? I gave her a gift, really, an escape from this horror, a quick and painless death. I'm merciful, though I'm no saint. I'm Marcus Titus also called Tempus. I'm older than I care to recall. I'm immortal, a vampire, and I'm also the destroyer of the entire world.

But it wasn't always this way.

I had a dream, a grandiose vision that would change the world forever, replacing it with a utopia undreamed. I believed my actions were justified. I planned it all out so carefully, decades of arcane research, countless sacrifices, and chose all the right pawns, but in the end it was human nature itself that threw a monkey wrench into the mix.

San Francisco Enquirer
April 13, 1968
Three Homeless Slain by the Zodiac Killer

Three bodies were discovered stacked in a bizarre triangle formation in Golden Gate Park this morning. A witness claimed a man wearing a long coat came upon four victims, stabbing wildly and ferociously without provocation. Allegedly there was a fourth victim, but to date no other body has been discovered.

I was so clever, choosing my pawns based upon their blood heritage, a few unnecessary theatrics and let the reporters create outlandish cover stories for my actions. It was so simple it was brilliant.

San Francisco Enquirer
April 23, 1968
Tragedy Strikes Veteran Demonstration

Early this morning, a peaceful Vietnam Veteran demonstration suddenly erupted in flames, claiming the lives of many and injuring several others. According to authorities, the accident was caused by a faulty gas line. In contrast to those claims, five victim's bodies were discovered, forming a star of sorts in the center of the flames. Authorities refuse to speculate, but according to Veteran's Affairs, at least one man in attendance remains unaccounted for.

A stabbing here, bit of arson there, a shovel used when I was feeling especially bastardly, always arranging the bodies in some ridiculous mockery of the occult, and all the while my true purpose would remain a mystery.

San Francisco Enquirer
May 3, 1968
Love-in Becomes Massacre

April Jones was admitted to the hospital this morning suffering from shock following a harrowing escape from death. April, a nineteen-year old co-ed, was invited to a party with several new friends. Everything was 'groovy' until the darkest hours before dawn, when a man in a black coat crashed through the door and began smashing people's brains in with a shovel! April swears she will always remember the killer's dark sadistic laughter while she hid in the closet, witnessing the methodical butchering of those poor hippies who had only gotten together for a good time...for the last time.

To be honest, I did enjoy some of the theatrics and may have taken it a bit too far on occasion.

San Francisco Enquirer
June 3, 1968
Zodiac Killer or Trilogy Slayer?

The most recent victim of violence in the city happening on a day ending in the number 'three' was found in a local television station. Three Media Technicians were discovered hanged from cables with cameras pointed at them and running. According to the access log, a fourth person was working that day. Authorities refuse to identify the person, but acknowledge there was no sign of the missing Media Technician and they have not ruled out he or she may be responsible. Police denied any association with the Zodiac Killer but new rumors speculate about a new killer, unofficially dubbed 'Trilogy Slayer.'

Sensational violence is so compatible with the media that if it didn't exist they would be forced to create it.
What was the point? The rituals necessary to change the past were very specific. You wonder if I ramble like a mad man, but I assure you

I'm as sane as you. I was a master of the Blackest Magic long before I was given the gift of eternal damnation and I'd seen the end of the world.

I knew no one was more capable of changing the horrid fate I had witnessed and I alone could save the world.

I did a helluva job.

Dust billowed in my wake as I approached the gates. Rusted, spiked remnants of car parts and rebar were welded to a rolling bar with two morons guarding it. I could kill them without a thought, but I have no desire to have an entire village of idiots chasing me with pitch forks and torches. A grubby diseased hand protrudes from strips of rotted fabric masquerading as clothing for the guard, ignoring the hand I lean in and whisper. His disgusting face splits with a sickening smile and with a mocking bow he steps back allowing me passage to the squalor that is Sweet Valley.

I hear his running feet scrape the earth as he bolts. Word spread quickly from one rat to the next until the vermin king is aware of the stranger and his fabulous treasure. Humans were everywhere scurrying, scrounging, stealing, and killing throughout this maze of dilapidated buildings that threatened to fall and crush you at any minute. I hate what humanity became. I walk on.

Gaudy signs scribbled and misspelled promised to relieve fools from their gold and any manner. *Wepins, Armers, Womins, Almost Fresh Food*, and on it went throughout the entire bazaar. Smashed together it created a maze within a maze where the falling buildings are your least concern. I make it to the bar just before the rats and their king burst into the room nearly stumbling all over each other in their retarded attempts to appear menacing. They failed.

I pretend to ignore them, hands flat and calm atop the bar. Scant moments pass. I sense their fear. My base instinct is to destroy and devour them all, but I have a much larger plan. Someone lets out a nervous bodily noise and the silence is broken.

125

"I hear you have somethin in particular there to trade." His accent is a mix of hillbilly and hooligan.

"I do." I purposely antagonize the slob.

"Well...let's see it afore my men run you out of town stranger." His breath smelled of moonshine and rot, but that was nothing compared to the stench of decay covering his limbs.

"I have a map."

"Who gives a crap? A map of what? You best do better than that!" Surely one of the fattest men I've seen since the world ended. His rolls glistening with sweat a mixture of fear and a total lack of hygiene.

"I happen to have of map and on this map is the location of two *Renegade Marauder* cache sites." He squirms and another drop of sickening sweat rolls down his protruding forehead. "On said map is also denoted the location of five Marauder ambushed vehicles, I believe to be yours, still full of juice and all carrying water, food, and all within a few miles from here and all less than one day dead. A smart man, a man of business, could make quite the profit and a smarter man could maybe even use this map to find the rest of the *Renegade Marauder* sites nearby. Are you a smart man?"

"That is one mother of a tale. How do I know you ain't lyin' or that you isn't the one who done the killin' and this is just some kinda trap?" I lower my goggles just long enough to make eye contact with the toad. As filthy as he was, I could still see his skin pale at the sight of my glistening black orbs ringed with fire. His bluster fades and I continue.

"Do you think for one second that I care about your infighting and incest? Use that tiny excuse for a brain rattling inside your head ape." I adjust my scarf and his rat eyes catch the gleam of steel beneath my coat." Did you see a vehicle when I arrived? No, so logically what would I want with fuel?" I make sure the movement briefly bares my black veined alabaster skin. "For that matter, my slovenly friend, what would I possibly want with water?" A small smile and my extended canines remove all shred of bravado from the cur. "Now we can either do business like gentlemen and I depart your lovely city as quietly as I entered or I shred all of your throats and gorge on your blood. The choice is yours."

"Wha...what would ya want in trade...?"

I describe the artifact I'm looking for. He has no idea what I'm talking about. At least he was smart enough not to try and lie. Another dead end, I'm not really surprised. As a consolation I give the location of the nearest scavenge site, thank him for his *hospitality*, and stride back out into the streets. They react quicker than I gave them credit. As I approach the gate a dozen rats are waiting for me weapons drawn. Apparently, the knowledge of one location was not enough in a world where gasoline and water are worth much more than a life.

I should've known.

Human greed and stupidity. The very reasons I sought the ritual in the first place.

My pawns traveled back in time to change three key events, altering the future significantly. I promised them power and wealth beyond their wildest dreams should they succeed and yet despite numerous blunderings and no small amount of luck, succeed they did. Knowing full well these covetous vampire bastards of mine would one day threaten my reign, I did the only sensible thing. I left them stranded in time.

The first stop was Venice, Italy December 28, 1481, to break up a meeting of the largest gathering of ancient vampires in history. Their mission was simply to convince three of the *Elders* not to sign a secret treaty that would push our kind forever in the shadows effectively surrendering the world to lesser beings. I could not allow this to transpire. This desperate act coupled with two more somewhat insignificant events eventually led to the end of my kind and I would do anything to prevent it. I was naive, arrogant, and blinded with power.

While clumsy as all hell, my pawns managed to bungle through their encounters relatively unscathed. Across rooftops vampires played a supernatural game of hide and seek, each trying to ascertain the other's intentions, each waiting for a reason to launch into combat. Naturally my young foreigners were being strategically led from one choice location to another by their local quarry until at last they landed in the viper's nest surrounded by over twenty vampires, all older, more skilled, and more powerful than they were.

Question after question, debate followed by threat, insult for insult matched and yet neither side gained any ground. Try as they might my time traveling vampires could not convince their ancestors of the truth. One by one their arguments were discounted as lies or trickery, from their style of dress to their accents and utter lack of civility. The latter was sarcasm of course.

Then the ridiculous happened. The hippy lit a smoke with his cigarette lighter.

This accidental and mundane demonstration of futuristic prowess was enough to convince three of the most powerful vampires in the world to not only walk away from decades of planning, but to spread the word that the precious treaty of fools must fail. Sometimes luck really is all you need.

Over the next few centuries a shadow feudal government ruled by vampires would spread baronies across the globe covertly dividing the human world among them. Remaining in the darkness and subtly pulling the strings of every country until the time was right for our ascension to open dominion. In every decision and evolution of human history a vampire steered the course. In hindsight the scientific progression of man became somewhat stagnant as those who live forever tend to ignore many of the desires of the flesh and priorities based on time have relatively low import to an immortal. This is not to say creativity was purposefully stunted, only accidentally retarded a bit.

Their first mission a success I transported them to the second of three pinnacle moments, this time November 22, 1781 to Ocracoke Island in the Carolinas. There they must prevent the ambush that caused the untimely death of Edward Teach, the pirate known as *Blackbeard*. Considering the vampire's natural dislike for sunlight, this was no simple task. Not being one to micro-manage I once again left the details to them.

Two ships were set to waylay Teach and his mere band of less than twenty men just after the good Captain had disembarked the bulk of his crew on another island for a much deserved shore leave. Historically, Blackbeard's ship ran aground while men led by Lieutenant Robert Maynard, hid in the belly of their ships, much like a *Trojan Horse*, and then butchered their greatly out-numbered foes to the man. This event would take a slightly differ-ent twist.

Somewhere in the chaos they concocted the plan to mind-control humans during daylight, managed to bring Blackbeard to them the night before the ambush, and even more ludicrous convinced him they were vampires sent back in time to make sure he survived. I will always wonder if his decision was based on his belief in the occult or just the last act of a man who knew Death was knocking on his door.

Lending their supernatural abilities they planted makeshift charges beneath the waves beaching the attacker's crafts and while the crew slept my children stealthily birthed several ghouls, humans temporarily imbued with vampiric strength and vitality. A few drops of vampire blood placed in their rum supply were all it took to transform the previously outnumbered force into a near unstoppable semi-undead host. I should have known this was not the greatest of plans.

Once again my pawns surprised me. My intent was only to let Teach live to disrupt the primary sea trades for a few decades while killing his opponent, Lieutenant Robert Maynard as a message of fear to the would-be Governors in the area. The rest was a bit accidental and incredibly unorthodox; the results however, remained conducive to my overall plans. Maynard's ships approached and one by one ran aground while *ghouled* pirates clambered the sides of their vessels from beneath the waves. Steel rang against steel and explosions of musket balls shattered the day and into the night skies. Blood soaked the boards and drained into the bay. In the end not a single of Blackbeard's pirates were lost and over sixty of her Majesty's Navy were slaughtered and Maynard's corpse hanged from the crow's nest.

Remember how I mentioned stranding them in time, well this was one of the primary reasons. One of my bastards took it upon himself to transform Edward Teach into one of our kind, creating perhaps the largest wave against the timeline imaginable. While it unmistakably altered my intended timeline, it did not destroy it and my plan moved forward.

Blackbeard would go on to create an undead fleet and rule the seas from the furthest edges of the ocean to every known port, civilized or otherwise. His actions would change the face of naval travel, trade, and actually prevent numerous human wars. He would no longer be known as just a tyrannical pirate, but a nautical genius whose innovations revolutionized sea travel and served as a deterrent to maritime hostilities. How the history books were just then completed urinated upon. Legends abound of his *Black Legion*, but none would ever dare entertain the truth and fewer still lived to tell of their encounters.

Initially, Blackbeard reacted accordingly with his newfound gifts. He plundered and raised hell. Somewhere in his unstoppable rampage it occurred to him that he was meant for something greater than this. On his own he reinvented the very concept of piracy and turned into more of a global vigilante attacking any potentially hostile ship on the seas. With every conquest he expanded his armada and his undead horde until there was no one able to confront him. It was then he declared himself King of the Seas demanding and receiving fealty from all the known world. The repercussions of this were the shockwave I felt on the timeline and yet strangely it fell into place neatly.

Their last assignment was an intervention of the most histori-cally inaccurate gun fight in American history — the *Shootout at the OK Corral*. On October 26, 1881 in Tombstone, Arizona...*the town too tough to die*...I always found that a curious misnomer. Wyatt Earp must die during the daylight and during the gun slinging. There were more than a few reasons why this act was important to the time continuum.

First and foremost had nothing to do with the man and every-thing to do with his offspring. Mordachi Earp, the eldest son of Wyatt, would grow to become one of the most powerful vampire slayers the world had ever known spawning an era of supernatu-ral hunters. His seed would be planted that very afternoon follow-ing the battle.

The other reason I must admit was purely selfish. While I rather enjoyed the *Kurt Russel* version I truly hated that *Kevin Costner* movie and this would make sure there would never be a reason to subject audiences to it.

The morons used a bit more cleverness this time, hopefully learning from their numerous recent mistakes. Using a combined knowledge of history and Hollywood...okay mostly just old western movies to be honest...anyway they devised a plan to isolate and follow a few select *cowboys* not originally involved in the shootout. The decision as to who those actual *cowboys* were centered primarily on actor's names from the movie *Tombstone*.

Once alone they wiped the drunk's mind and implanted sug-gestions of sabotage and assassination, of course triggered exactly at the same time as the firefight. The debate over the actual trigger, as to whether it should be an audible, verbal, or visual finally gave way to common sense.

They knew what time the shootout took place and all they had to do was hope their brainwashees could tell time. Luck be damned. Their plan resulted in four additional unwitting gun-slingers who filled Wyatt Earp with more lead than any doctor would care to count. Due to the confusion each of the mind-wiped cowboys ended up shot three ways to hell by *Doc Holiday* and *Virgil Earp*.

I mentioned there were other reasons that forced my decision to never returning them to my present. Despite their auspicious victories, they alone knew my plans and therefore the potential seed for betrayal existed.

Sure, I thought of bringing them back just to destroy them, but this seemed to be the simpler way to sever ties. Even if they somehow managed to survive the next few centuries, they would have no idea how to find me.

I did mention I was arrogant.

The next century greeted our kind with a grand opportunity, one that would conclude with our even grander demise. Slowly down through the centuries the shadow governments prevented one war after another, stalled many humane innovations as their attentions were focused more on creating and maintaining an underground blood network and labs capable of mass production of synthetic blood.

War, apartheid, democracy, disease, and even slavery were all but abolished replaced by an undead dystopia in which all the needs of the people were attended to, there were no rich and no poor, everyone worked for the better of the community, and all it required was a small blood donation from its citizens on a monthly basis. In return everyone lived full comfortable lives where hedonism and work ethics merged to a sweet ballet of perfection. Yet even with all of this perfect, an ape would surely argue that they remained slaves to their vampire masters.

You simply cannot please some *people*.

Each continent was divided into feudal style baronies, boundaries long since defined from the shadows, eliminating all country biases and creating united land masses under one central ruler. Each barony governed by a Baron who was in turn governed by the Chancellor, elected once per century from among each Barony to prevent stagnation of the line.

The rules of conduct and trade were ratified across each ocean and enforced by the Black Legion. Humans tended to their dark lord's demands and were well rewarded for their service. It was truly a caste system based on theories of Charles Darwin and Thomas More with a bit of H.G. Wells for good measure. Simple, clean, efficient; no wonder it had to be destroyed.

While the world finally operated at what appeared to be optimal efficiency within its core, a cancer formed. Greed, no matter how good some have *it* there will always be those who believe they deserve *it* more, but never want to actually put forth any real effort. Why create when it is easier to destroy, later mimic, and eventually call it your own.

Escaped or missing donors began to be a problem near the end of the twentieth century. At first no one really noticed or cared. There were stockpiles of blood all around the globe. A few missing blood bags could not make a difference. The number of donors continued to decrease and it was evident that many of the humans simply were not there, but still nothing was done. A few *alarmists* like myself tried to make the rulers see the truth, but not until it became a frequent conversation piece did it lose its charm and had to be reconsidered a threat. I hate politics.

Initially there were no signs of the missing donors and rumors of a government hoax or some such conspiracy circulated. You simply cannot argue logic with emotional beings. The centuries of fat living had made my fellow vampires complacent, lethargic even, and it sickened me. Debate after debate as to what needed to be done was followed by argument after argument regarding the correct level of force to use.

While they discussed the most effective and least intrusive plan to never exist the unthinkable happened; a vampire was found dead, his head removed and stuffed with garlic. Logic and reason died with that poor undead guard.

The missing donors were now branded *terrorists* with bounties placed on their heads. Considering no one really knew which humans were responsible this resulted in the summary execution, accidental dismemberment, and occasional disembowelment of countless apes.

Some felt the initial reaction of unrestrained violence was enough while others believed a swift decisive act of *overkill* would quell any form of uprising. Their stupidity only made the matter worse, much, much worse.

Amidst streets run red with blood and vampires, plasma processing centers all over the world exploded in flaming showers of crimson rain. Accidental or not the nearby laboratories were also engulfed in the chaos.

Synthetic blood, fire, samples of every disease known to man and a few unknowns as well, mixed creating toxic blood clouds that spread across the land faster than anyone could react. As it flows it mutates seemingly taking on sentience destroying all in its path. Crops withered and rotted, rivers turned to poison, living creatures dying by the herds, animals and man alike.

Once again their initial assessments completely wrong, my kind assumed themselves immune to the plague clouds. Vampires were not so immortal as they once believed. The virus burned at the blood cells making it impossible to heal, creating horrid disfigurements, scars, and in most cases true death. It grew from within literally cooking the host alive before bursting through scorched pores on to the next victim spreading faster than the common flu. Many of us fled underground to sleep out the plague, with hopes of awakening to a less hostile land, but the apes were resourceful and we had told them too many of our secrets. One by one my kind were hunted in their barrows and destroyed while they slumber. A new form of rebellion rose from the ashes of death.

This act could not go unanswered. Brutality on both sides was quickly discarded as a notion of practicality and each developed more ingenious ways to destroy the other. Now the battles raged above and below ground until numbers on both sides became so diminished neither was certain if the other still existed. *Scorched Earth* became the battle cry on all fronts and highways gave way to scattered outposts, loners roaming where thousands of vehicles once traveled, blackened craters to remind us of power plants, cracked earth a mockery of the once lush forests or farmlands. Death smiled back from every turn. Any semblance of an intelligent society raped and discarded.

It was clear what I must do. I needed to unravel time once again, it was the only way. Clearly. Perhaps my initial calculations were off, somewhere I made a minor mistake, no, impossible, more likely those bastards of mine found a way to plant seeds of dissension in my Garden of Eden.

It was at that moment, between animalistic survival instincts, mindless rage, and bloodthirsty slaughter that a kind of Zen came over me and I realized my amulet was missing. I tore every place and person apart anywhere near my hiding lairs and beyond, fruitless, bloody, and useless. The only artifact powerful enough to open the time stream and the only way to...to...fix things...again...and I lost it!

The rats pour at me from several directions. I meet their charges faster than they can even think severing limbs, slashing arteries, and crushing skulls. I move through them quickly dissecting their ranks like a surgeon and leaving a trail of blood in my wake.

They swing axes, spears, and torches at me a few even hold crucifixes soon discovering that none of it mattered. Someone shot me! I had not considered they would have firearms and more importantly, ammunition. He dies next with a clean decapitation in the same motion I take his pistol and put a bullet in the mouth of the fat rat king. In the end I do as I promised. I slit their throats and gorge on their blood.

A few other Sweet Valley denizens almost muster the courage to stop me, but by the twentieth or so butchered rat they scurry away to their holes. I casually shake off the grime and pick a few pieces of flesh from my coat as I walk through the gates as calmly as when I entered.

If I despise them so much why do I continue my search? If I hold civilization, human and vampire alike, in such contempt why would I even contemplate scouring a dead planet like an obsessed archaeologist? Perhaps I have a hero complex, or rather a dark sort of anti-hero complex.

Again, my former colleagues could surely debate this to the end of time, which for them has passed, but in the end it's quite simple.

This future was neither the vision I tried to thwart nor the dystopia I envisioned.

This was a complete and other catastrophe on its own and I alone held the wisdom to correct it.

Once I had the amulet...I would be Time's Master again and make my little ingrates pay for ruining my dream.

I did mention I was arrogant, right?

ABOUT THE WRITERS

Dana Bell is a Colorado writer. Her first novel 'Winter Awakening' from WolfSinger Publications is available on Amazon. She has stories in several anthologies, listed on her fanfiction profile page, and poems in magazines. She lives with her husband David Luperti who is a nature photographer and three cats Sammy, Maximillian and Adara. Building and decorating doll houses is her main hobby along with writing fanficiton under the name Dragonlots.

See more of her work at: www.fanfiction.net/~dragonlots.

Vincenzo Bilof is an educator who lives in Detroit, Michigan. He was awarded the "2011 Literary Achievement Award" by SNM Horror Magazine after publishing 8 consecutive stories for their monthly contests. His work appears in the anthologies "Bonded by Blood: Scarlet Sunset" by SNM Publishing, "Frightmares" by Dark Moon Books, and "Book of the Dead 6" by Living Dead Press. His horror stories also appear in 6 anthologies from Open Casket Press, including "Gnomes of the Dead" and "Mutant Apocalypse." The story appearing in Zombie Tales titled "Hero's End" features the protagonist, Lenir, from Vincenzo's zombie-apocalypse novel "Under a Red Sun," forthcoming

Robert O. Boras is a lodger and writer of all things fantastical. He's currently working on his first novella, "Trappe Street," which is writing on an old typewriter in the spare room of a kindly old woman. He hopes to publish it as an e-book in the next few months, if the world does not end first.

Tony Garcia is a reclusive hermit living somewhere in the mountains of Arizona. He combines his love of multiple genres ranging from Dark Fantasy to Horror to bring his imagination to life. While writing, editing, and reviewing works for several years, this is his first published Horror story. He currently works for the US Army designing training simulations and his primary literary influences include Robert E. Howard, H.P. Lovecraft, and Michael Moorcock.

Anthony Giangregorio is the author of 45 novels, almost all of them about zombies, and has edited over 40 anthologies and books. His work has appeared in Dead Science & Metahumans vs. the Undead by Coscomentertainment, Dead Worlds: Undead Stories Volumes 1-7, and Wolves of War by Library of the Living Dead Press. He also has stories in End of Days: An Apocalyptic Anthology Vol. 1-5, the Book of the Dead series Vol. 1-6 by LDP, Zombie Zoology by Severed Press, and two anthologies with Pill Hill Press. He's also the creator of the 10 book action/zombie series titled Deadwater and the apocalyptic series Warriors of the Apocalypse. His action/horror novel Dead Rage is being optioned for a movie at this time. Visit him on Facebook

Gabino Iglesias is a writer and journalist currently working on his PhD in journalism. His non-fiction work has appeared in The New York Times, the Austin Post, Business Today magazine, San Antonio magazine and many other publications. His fiction has appeared in Bizarro Central, MicroHorror, El Nuevo Dia and a few anthologies that will be released in 2012, including The Plastic Electric Baby Jesus and other Bizarro Zombie Tales. He lives in Austin, TX.

Christopher Nadeau is the author of "Dreamers at Infinity's Core" and has over two dozen published short stories in such august publications as The Horror Zine, Sci-Fi Short Story Magazine, Ghostlight Magazine and many more. He was interviewed as part of Suspense Radio's up and coming authors program and collaborated on two "machinima" films with UK animator Celestial Elf called "The Gift," and 'The Deerhunter's Tale," both of which can be viewed on YouTube. His novel "Echoes of Infinity's Core" is slated for a 2012 release. An active member of the Great Lakes Association of Horror Writers, Chris Resides in Southeastern Michigan with his wife Lorie and two petulant long-hair Chihuahuas.

Marc Shemmans is a writer from Birmingham, UK. He has had several stories published in a variety of magazines and anthologies from both sides of the Atlantic. At this moment in time he is writing an apocalyptic novella, a horror short story and several screenplays. He is hoping they will find homes as soon as they are finished.

R P Steeves is a former teacher and a writer who specializes in the fantastic. His first novel, an urban fantasy tale of paranormal detection, "Misty Johnson, Supernatural Dick in Capitol Hell" is available in print and ebook formats, and its sequel is due out in 2012.

Follow his blog and learn of his upcoming horror, fantasy and pulp adventure titles at http://www.rpsteeves.com

Jonathan Templar lives in Cheshire, England. His recent published and soon to be published work includes short stories in Open Casket Press's collection "Dead Christmas" ('Secret Santa'), the shared world anthology "World's Collider" ('Basher'), Smart Rhino's collection "Zippered Flesh" ('Marvin's Angry Angel'), and in Wicked East Press' "Bedtime Stories for Girls," but nobody believes him when he mentions that.

Contact him at www. jonathantemplar.com

HORROR CARNIVAL
Edited by Anthony Giangregorio

Step right up, folks, the Horror Carnival is about to begin!

We have a great show in store for you this evening.

Ghouls, monsters, zombies, vampires and serial killers, all rolled up into one massive show. Tales that will leave you wanting more yet leave you oh so fulfilled.

The rides are cheap, the stories tall, so grab some cotton candy and popcorn and enjoy yourself. Tickets are five for a dollar!

But please read all disclaimers before entering the fairgrounds.

Horror Carnival is not responsible for any dismemberment or loss of organs during your visit, nor are we liable if any family member is slain while participating in one of the attractions. So come on in…if you dare!

CREATURE FEATURE: A MONSTER ANTHOLOGY
Edited by Anthony Giangregorio

Giant squirrels, massive zombies, killer trees and marauding severed heads are just a few of the twisted tales of creatures you will find inside this anthology.

So let your imagination free and embrace what isn't real.

For perhaps monsters are real, and it is you that does not truly exist.

RATS
By Anthony Giangregorio

Killer black rats the size of dogs are roaming the streets and no one is aware of their existence.

Wild dogs, the authorities warn. Stay indoors and all will be fine.

Domenic Salvatore soon finds himself in the middle of a cover-up of epic proportions; where no one will believe the truth.

And why would they? After all, he's just a kid.

What no one knows is that the rats have taken on a taste for human meat, a particular kind of meat actually…young flesh…the flesh of children.

As the kids are hunted one by one, killed and dragged off into the night to be devoured, Domenic realizes that it's only a matter of time before he's next.

Something evil stalks the town of Wakefield, Mass…and it's hungry.

BIGFOOT TALES
Edited by Mark Christopher
The elusive Bigfoot has been a mystery for years.

Truth or hoax? No one knows for sure and perhaps never will.

So does this creature of the forest truly exist? Is there really a missing link that ties together man with his ape ancestors?

Or is it all simply a figment of the imagination.

DEAD CHRISTMAS: A ZOMBIE ANTHOLOGY
Edited by Anthony Giangregorio
Share the most special time of the year with someone you love, or better yet, with an animated corpse!

The living dead love Christmas. Whether they're hanging their entrails like garland, using severed heads like stockings, or hanging body parts like ornaments, even zombies enjoy the most wonderful time of the year.

Santa Claus isn't immune to the walking dead, either.

Zombie elves, killer reindeer and undead hordes, all seek to share in the joy of the holiday . . . and tear Santa apart and feed on his flesh.

So when you grab last year's fruitcake to re-gift to Aunt Martha, just make sure to bring a shotgun, too. Because for all you know, your aunt has turned into an undead flesh-eater, and if the shotgun won't kill her, the fruitcake most assuredly will.

SURVIVAL HORROR: A ZOMBIE STORY
By Paul Johnson
A new game show is sweeping the world. In the UK, contestants are lining up at the Mile High Tower for their chance to win £10,000,000,000. Nathan Baxter is in that line. Broke and desperate for money to support his family, he edges closer to his destiny.

Stay alive for an hour, that's all he has to do. But so far no one has won or even come close. Can Nathan kill enough zombies to put his wife and five-year-old son on easy street for a few years? Or can he shock the nation and win the show.

UNDEAD PRESS

Where the Dead Never Sleep

UNDEADPRESS.COM

CREATURE FEATURE
A MONSTER ANTHOLOGY

EDITED BY
ANTHONY GIANGREGORIO

VICTORY OF THE DEAD

ANTHONY GIANGREGORIO

THE BOOK OF CANNIBALS

KISS THE COOK

Longoria Grill

EDITED BY
ANTHONY
GIANGREGORIO